ONCE IN A
HALF MOON

Other books by Fran McNabb:

A Light in the Dark

ONCE IN A HALF MOON

•

Fran McNabb

AVALON BOOKS
NEW YORK

Published by Thomas Bouregy & Co., Inc.
160 Madison Avenue, New York, NY 10016

Library of Congress Cataloging-in-Publication Data

McNabb, Fran.
  Once in a half moon / Fran McNabb.
      p.   cm
  ISBN 978-0-8034-9895-2 (hardcover : acid-free paper)
  I. Title

PS3613.C5856O63   2008
813'.6—dc22   2007047383

PRINTED IN THE UNITED STATES OF AMERICA
ON ACID-FREE PAPER
BY HADDON CRAFTSMEN, BLOOMSBURG, PENNSYLVANIA

To two wonderful ladies: My mother, Manda, who taught me the meaning of unconditional love, and Bobbie Thibodeaux, my mentor and friend, whose encouragement and guidance I'll always value.

Chapter One

"Chum, poles, and every kind of lure you could possibly want. You name it, we got it. My boat has everything a fisherman . . ."

Nikki Clark listened to the gray-haired boat captain extol the merits of his sleek charter vessel. She stood on a pier in the harbor and tried to ignore the stiff wind that sent her hair flying, holding it away from her face with one hand. Waves crashed against the concrete piers, dampening her clothes but not her spirits. Nothing could take away the excitement of being back home and working at her new job.

The unexpected northwester churned up the normally serene waters of the Mississippi Sound. Not good for the midsummer tourist business, but the lousy weather gave the boat captains time to make necessary repairs to their vessels and their equipment.

Nikki took advantage of having the boats in the harbor. For most of the day she'd been introducing herself to the men who would take her hotel guests out among the barrier islands, where they would reel in snapper, cobia, and redfish.

Nikki glanced at the time on her cell phone. Her first day at the harbor was coming to an end, and she still had one more boat captain to meet. With a diplomatic air honed on her last job in public relations, she cut the conversation short and stepped away from the vessel.

At the end of the pier a gray pelican crouched next to a piling to shield itself from the wind. As Nikki neared, it lifted its big body with outstretched wings, then landed a few feet away.

"I'm sorry, big fellow. Didn't mean to scare you." She watched the pelican waddle past several boats until it found protection behind another piling. Unlike the pelican, the last thing Nikki wanted to do was to hide from the elements. Even if it meant wild hair and damp attire, the wind refreshed her spirits. She loved being back home on the coast.

She looked at her list of prospective charter vessels. *The Half-Moon*. Strange name for a boat, she thought, but the name of the captain intrigued her even more— Preston. It sent a warm sensation through her chest. Her best friend's husband was a Preston. Was there a family connection?

She corrected that thought. Her *former* best friend. Nikki couldn't call her a best friend any longer, not when she hadn't heard from MaryAnn in years.

Still, being friends with MaryAnn's former husband shouldn't have been put on hold all these years. A tiny twinge of guilt reminded her she hadn't called Russ Preston to let him know she'd be back on the coast. She made a promise to herself to call Russ tonight. Or tomorrow. But soon. She could use the friendship of someone from her past, especially someone who had been as close as a brother years ago.

As she stepped onto a smaller finger pier and walked under the sign of THE HALF-MOON CHARTERS, she wondered how she and Russ had let their friendship slide away after all they'd been through together.

Looking up from her clipboard, she smiled. "Hi, I'm Nikki—" The rest of the introduction stuck in her throat. "Oh, my gosh. Russ. It's you. You're Captain Preston."

Russ stood on the clean white deck of a beautiful charter boat, his legs spread apart. Wearing khaki shorts and a white fishing shirt that clung to his tanned body in the wind, he reminded Nikki of Neptune standing amid the ocean's fury.

For a moment she thought her eyes were deceiving her, but then he spoke, and the deep voice could belong to no one else.

"The last time I checked, I was still Captain Preston." He winked at her, then smiled. "Nikki Clark. What are you doing down here in this weather?"

Seeing Russ sent her brain into a tailspin. It took her a moment to remember why she had been hopping on and off boats all day. "Uh, it's my new job. But I could ask you the same thing." She waved her arms, indicating the boat. "Is this yours?"

Another smile spread across his rugged face, a face she'd always thought handsome. During their college days he and MaryAnn had made a stunning couple. Like herself, he was now more than a few years older, but his broad shoulders and his well-toned arms and legs still showed signs of regular workouts—or maybe just plain hard work.

"Yep," he answered, and he looked around at his boat with pride. "It's been my life for about three years now."

"Your life? What happened to your accounting business?"

"Things change, Nikki." Russ wiped his hands with a towel, then tossed it to the top of a tool chest. "Why don't you come on board? You can tell me why you're here talking to salty dog fishermen, and I'll tell you what's happened to me lately."

"Deal." She held her clipboard close to her body once more, but before she could take yet another carefully placed step down to a boat deck, Russ reached out a hand.

The years fell away. The warmth of his hand through the roughened skin swelled her chest with memories of years gone by, when MaryAnn and Russ and she and her ex-husband, David, were inseparable.

As soon as her foot reached the deck, Russ pulled her into a brotherly embrace. His ragged breath warmed her cheek. She knew her presence here today was likely throwing him back into a black hole of memories too. Maybe that's why she hadn't called to let him know she was moving back home. Being together would dredge up the past for both of them.

"It's good to see you," he whispered into her hair as he hugged her close. "You've been away too long."

Not wanting the moment of familiarity to end, Nikki relaxed against his chest and savored his embrace.

Finally, with a tight hug and a loud exhale of breath, he moved his hands down her arms and held her at arm's length. "You look good."

Nikki stepped away. "Still the Southern gentleman, aren't you? I appreciate the compliment, but I'm afraid the years have taken their toll."

He chuckled. "What mirror have you been looking into?"

Nikki backed against the railing. "The truth mirror, that's what."

Russ shook his head. "I've learned we see in that mirror pretty much only what we want to see."

"We do, huh?" She laughed, then got serious. "I don't know, Russ. I want to see that young woman I used to be, but the only face that keeps popping up is this thirty-five-year-old one. Sometimes it looks back with the eyes of a woman much older."

Russ nodded. "Yeah, I know what you mean. I don't

always like what I see staring back at me either. But you know what? We've both been through more than our share of problems over the years. The kids we were when we walked across that university stage for our degrees vanished a long time ago." He raised his eyebrows and grinned. "Maybe that's not a bad thing."

Nikki loved the twinkle in his eye. Even during their college years, when things seemed overwhelming, she could always count on Russ' positive outlook. It was still present today, even after all the hard times he'd been through.

She exaggerated a shudder. "You're so right. I'd hate to think I had to relive some of those years, but I wouldn't mind seeing a little of that younger me."

Russ surprised her. He lifted her chin with one finger. "You don't have anything to worry about. You and MaryAnn were the prettiest girls on that campus, and you haven't lost a bit of that beauty."

"Lying doesn't become you, Captain Preston. I haven't been called beautiful in many years, but I'll remember your words when I look in that morning mirror again."

"If the men in Chicago haven't lavished you with compliments, obviously they're blind."

She opened her mouth to tell him there hadn't been any men in her life since the divorce, but at that moment the bottom of the cabin door flew open, and a huge mountain of black fur lunged forward.

Nikki shrieked and jumped behind one of the fishing chairs. "Good gracious! Is that a dog or a bear?"

Russ laughed. "That's Hammerhead, and he's definitely a dog."

Hammerhead stiffened into alert mode, his shaggy black hair standing up on the scruff of his neck. With one side of his upper lip raised to show his teeth, he growled.

"It's okay, Hammerhead. Nikki's a friend."

The dog's black eyes seemed to see right through her. Her heart pumped in triple-time. "Uh, I like dogs, but he doesn't look like he likes me."

"He's fine. He's really just a big teddy bear."

"Teddy bear, huh?"

Russ stooped down. Hammerhead eyed Nikki a little longer before giving in to Russ' coddling. The dog's guard disappeared as he slumped against Russ' leg and waited for the expected pat on the head. He licked Russ' hand and wagged his tail.

"You can pet him if you'd like, and if you scratch behind his ears, he'll love you forever."

Nikki would rather take a dive into the murky water of the harbor than to pet a dog that looked as if his favorite meal was raw meat and nails, but she wasn't about to show the animal how scared she was of him.

"Hi, Hammerhead." Nikki stooped down next to Russ and the dog, then spoke in what she hoped was a cool, calm voice. "I'll bet you have no trouble keeping people off your master's boat. I can't imagine anyone trying to get onto this boat with you here."

Hammerhead's stare softened as he allowed Nikki to rub his head. She thought she even heard a sigh.

"Yep. He's the cheapest and best watchman around the harbor." Russ spoke directly to the dog. "Of course, you took your sweet time getting out on deck just now. What if this lady had been a robber instead of an old friend?"

Hammerhead ignored his master's light scolding and continued to rub his head against Russ' leg.

Russ shook his head. "Usually no one gets onto this finger pier if he doesn't know someone in the group. He looks about as ferocious as one of those hammerhead sharks we pull in, but under that mound of fur, he's really sweet. He was a stray. He wandered up to the harbor one day. We've all adopted him, but my boat's the lucky one he chose to make his home."

With one last pat to the dog's head, Russ stood up. Nikki did the same.

"Why don't you come into the cabin out of this wind? I'll get us a drink."

"Oh, no. A little wind's not running me inside. I'd rather sit outside. I can't get enough of this view."

"I understand that." Russ looked down at Hammerhead. "You keep Nikki company. I'll be back in a minute."

Nikki watched Russ step into the cabin, then turned back to make sure the dog wasn't in attack mode again. He wasn't. Instead, he'd flopped down against one of the fishing chairs, never taking his eyes off her.

"Mind if I share one of these chairs, Hammerhead? We can use this time to bond until Russ gets back."

Hammerhead's black eyes didn't indicate anything near a bonding response, but Nikki turned one of the large white chairs, wiped the water out of it with Russ' towel, then sat down.

Russ, a charter boat captain. She nodded. He fit the role. He'd been the intelligent, levelheaded guy in their group of friends. No one was surprised when he'd gone on to get his CPA and open up a thriving business, but even with his patience and calm disposition, Nikki always felt he had a yearning to do something outside the confines of an office.

Yep, she could see where he'd make a good charter boat captain, but she wondered what had prompted the change in careers.

Taking a deep breath, she relaxed against the head-rest. What would he say about *her* career change and her move back home?

She glanced down at the dog. "Russ looks like he has his life back in control. How can I tell him that mine is in shambles?"

Leaning over, she scratched behind the dog's big ears. "I'm tempted to dump my problems on him. I could use a little of that big heart of his."

Hammerhead inhaled a deep breath that sounded like a snore, turned his head, and ignored her.

"You know what kind of a man he is. He took you in." She giggled. "Anyone who'd take in a dog as ugly as you must be a decent human. Don't you agree?"

The sigh that escaped her lips was almost as loud as

the dog's. Russ had been through so much in the last few years, she hated to burden him with her problems.

She thought about the foursome they had been in college. She and David. MaryAnn and Russ.

They'd all been so idealistic back then. So full of dreams. For so long she'd thought that Russ and MaryAnn lived a storybook existence, with their daughter, Libby, coming along after four years of marriage.

But dreams had a way of fading. Nikki's dream of a love-filled marriage had shattered a little more with each of David's extramarital escapades.

Russ and MaryAnn's dreams had ended abruptly after the car accident that put Libby into the hospital and MaryAnn on a course into the arms of a doctor.

Russ had been right. Things did change.

She relaxed against the cool vinyl seat and knew she could use some of Russ' kind words right now, but she prayed she could stick to her plan. She was determined to get this job under way and settle into her new apartment before she sought the comfort and help of her old friend.

Maybe not leaning on Russ wasn't the smartest thing to do, but neither had staying with her husband been after she'd realized her marriage wasn't working. It still hurt to realize she hadn't been able to do anything to keep her thirteen-year marriage together. In deep thought, she crossed her arms and hugged herself.

Hammerhead barely opened his eyes when Russ

stepped out of the cabin, but his tail beat against the side railing of the boat.

"Here we go." Russ stepped next to Nikki's chair and handed her a can in an insulated holder. "Coldest cola in the harbor."

Smiling up at him, she took the drink. "Thanks, Russ. Anything wet would taste good right now."

Russ turned the other oversized fishing chair toward her, then sat down. She sensed a tenseness in him that hadn't been there moments ago. Even with the overcast sky, he'd donned his sunglasses, but they couldn't hide the tiny worry lines in his forehead and around his eyes. With him sitting so close to her, she now saw the speckling of gray in his chestnut hair.

He didn't lean back but sat on the edge of the chair, feet spread apart. Holding his cola in one hand, he leaned slightly to pat the dog.

"So, how is it you ended up on this pier today?" His words pulled her into the present. "Have you moved home?"

She took a long swallow and nodded. "Yep. This place is special to me. Mom and Dad are out on the West Coast now, but this is where I wanted to come when I made the decision to move. You know what they say about the road always leading to home when you need it most." She swallowed hard. "I guess I'm in need."

Russ nodded slowly. "Aren't we all?"

His lips curved up in a smile, but the mirth didn't

reach his eyes. She wanted to wipe away the hint of sadness she saw there. She cleared her throat. "The company I was working for in Chicago lost its overseas contract. They started cutting back. I hadn't gotten a pink slip yet, but I could tell it was coming."

"I'm sorry."

"No, don't be. I think it was a good thing. I knew I had to make some changes in my life, but you know how it is. It's hard to move out of your comfort zone."

This time he nodded but said nothing.

"Anyway, I'd been reading the local paper online, and I saw this ad. To make a long story short, I applied, got the job, and moved within three weeks. So, here I am."

"Yep, here you are—without even calling me to say you were on your way." He raised an eyebrow over his shades.

Nikki grimaced. "Guilty as charged. It happened fast. Too fast. I planned to call you as soon as I got set-tled." She hesitated. "This move was something I had to do on my own."

He nodded as if he understood. Hadn't he always un-derstood her, even more than David had?

"And what is this job?" Russ asked. "You selling fishing tackle?"

She surprised herself by chuckling. "No, not fishing tackle. I work for the Hotel Royale. I'm in charge of scheduling charter boats for fishing excursions for our guests. Sometimes I'll help with the golf packages as well. It'll be a new service provided by the hotel."

"Really? Sounds great. Most of the hotels just leave our literature in a display case somewhere."

"I think it's going to be a really good job. It gives me a chance to be out of the office and enjoy the coastline. I missed the beach and water so much. We had the lakes, of course, but I miss this." She looked around and smiled.

"I don't think I'd ever be able to leave."

When she looked back at Russ, she saw him staring out over the channel that led to the nearby islands. "I want my Libby to enjoy growing up with the beauty I had around me."

"And how is Libby? It's been way too long since I've seen her."

Russ beamed. "She's doing great. I think she's had her last surgery. She's about as normal as any little nine-year-old could be."

"I can't wait to see her. I could use some Libby hugs."

"I think I can share a few with you. She'll be thrilled to see you."

Nikki nodded, again feeling the guilt that always came from letting life get in the way of those she loved. After the accident that sent the little girl into multiple surgeries on her legs, Nikki had flown down to be with MaryAnn and her family.

But then her own life had screamed for attention as she realized just how much David enjoyed her time away.

She shook away the tension that those memories

always caused. "I hope she remembers me. It's been years since I've seen her."

"Yeah. Time kind of got away from us, didn't it?"

"Unfortunately, yes." She changed the subject. "So, you do this charter boating full-time? When did this happen?"

He shrugged. "I guess right after I last saw you. During and after the divorce I tried to keep my office open, but I was distracted. Between meeting with lawyers, fighting over the settlement with MaryAnn, judges, and then the endless surgeries for Libby, I didn't do my clients justice."

"I know that must've been hard on you."

Russ nodded. He got quiet and took a moment before continuing. "I couldn't leave Libby alone, even though my family tried to help. I lost clients. I don't blame them. I tried to keep up by working at night, but I couldn't. Something had to give, and it certainly wasn't going to be my daughter and what she needed."

"You're a good daddy. You always have been. She's a lucky little girl to have you."

His gaze dropped to the floor. "I try to be, but she needs more than me." He looked up. "She's asking about her mother again lately. How do you tell a little girl that her mother just up and left her?"

What could she say? Libby was only four when Russ found himself having the responsibility of raising his child by himself.

She had to ask, even though she was afraid she knew the answer. "Does MaryAnn ever come to see her?"

He shook his head. "No, she's still angry that the judge gave me full custody. She's being spiteful. I guess it doesn't matter to her that Libby's the one being hurt."

She watched him shrug off the bad moment before he continued. "Okay. You said you'd tell me all the gory details about why you ended up here and the latest with David."

She grimaced. "Can it wait? I'll tell you everything later if you let me off the hook right now. The last thing I want to talk about is your friend David."

Russ harrumphed. "My friend, huh? If he were still my friend, I wouldn't have had to ask you what happened."

Now it was her turn to shrug. "He changed, Russ. He wasn't the same guy you ran around with in high school and college. Or maybe he was, and I was too blind to see it. Sometimes I wondered who I married."

She pulled her cell phone out of her pocket and glanced at the time. "I've got to get back to the office. Can we talk about David another time?"

"Sure. At least I know I'll get to see you again."

"Oh, you'll see me again. I'm putting *The Half-Moon* at the top of my charter list."

Chapter Two

After taking a detour to a local deli and to his mother's to pick up Libby, Russ headed home, where he and Libby ate shrimp po'boys and washed them down with root beers. Libby turned on her computer at the little desk he'd built her just last Christmas. He flipped on the news, but as he stared at the screen, he realized he had no idea what he was hearing.

His mind was on Nikki. He relived every minute she'd been on his boat. She'd been right. They'd changed since their college days together. So much had happened to both of them.

She was still as attractive as ever but with an air of maturity and sophistication that became her. Her auburn hair was as gorgeous as it always had been, but—she'd been right—she couldn't hide the stress beneath the surface beauty. He sensed it. He and Nikki had always had a way of understanding each other, even when the others did not.

He remembered how their college friends had originally thought he and Nikki were a couple. They weren't. He had loved MaryAnn, and Nikki loved David.

Still, Nikki was always there when he needed help.

He smiled, thinking about the time when MaryAnn was consumed with wedding plans while he was struggling with the idea of going back to school to get his master's degree. He'd been standing on the balcony of his small apartment, watching MaryAnn rush down the stairs with bags of wedding stuff. At the bottom she turned to him and yelled up, "Call Nikki. She'll know what to do."

MaryAnn had been right. He and Nikki had talked for over an hour that day, and when he'd gotten off the phone, he knew he had to send in the paperwork to enter graduate school. She'd convinced him that if he went back to school, he and MaryAnn would find the money to make ends meet.

"You have to do what your heart tells you," Nikki had told him. "If you don't, you'll always wonder if things could've been different. You and MaryAnn love each other. You'll be even closer by the time she helps you get through the next year of classes. Sharing hardship brings a couple together."

Her words had made everything so clear that day. The wedding took place, and instead of buying a house as most of their friends were doing, he and MaryAnn moved into his small off-campus apartment. The first years of their marriage had been wonderful, but before he knew it, the years had flown by, and things changed.

In deep thought, he finished his sandwich. Time *was* flying, but he was managing to survive. He looked over at Libby. Thank goodness for her. He'd filled his life with his boat and with his little girl, and he worked so hard that at night he went to sleep with no trouble.

But tonight—tonight he knew things would be different. Something had happened today that had confused him. Nikki had done nothing to indicate anything but friendship, and yet something about her had stirred emotions in him that had lain dormant for years.

By the end of her first week on the job Nikki was running her new office alone. She'd booked six fishing charters and one night cruise, but *The Half-Moon* hadn't been available. She'd talked with Russ a couple of times over the phone, but with both of them so busy, they hadn't gotten together.

"No excuses," she mumbled as she shuffled through her list of to-do items. Resolving to fix the omission of not having seen Libby and Russ yet, she put them at the top of her list. She'd call him today.

Feeling better, she opened the folder with the names of future hotel guests who had requested fishing charters or golf packages. Within minutes she had coupled the names with possible openings, but before she had time to pick up the phone, the office door flew open after one quick, hard knock.

To her delight, Russ strolled in.

"Russ! I was just thinking about you and Libby."

"Were you now?"

"Yep. You and Libby got put onto the top of my list. I can't believe we've both been so busy, we haven't gotten together."

"Well, I think things are about to settle down for me again. I finished my last trip with a convention that's been in town. Maybe now I'll have some breathing room."

She walked around her desk to him. He gave her a quick peck on the cheek before he propped one hip up on her desk. "I was in the neighborhood, and I thought I'd come down to see you. How's the new job treating you?"

Dressed in a pair of khaki shorts, a pullover shirt, and his boat shoes, Russ looked good. He'd lost the tenseness she'd detected on his boat that first day.

"The job's going great." She knew she beamed, but she didn't try to hide her joy. "I can't believe I've been so busy, but I love it. It's all I can do to keep up with the requests."

"That's one of the reasons I'm here. I think I can take on a few of your charters in the next week."

"Hey, great." She flipped through her scheduling book. "I have one that just came up for tomorrow. You can have it if you want."

"Put me down. How many will be on board?"

Russ turned into a professional captain, asking questions he'd need to perfect the trip. She gave him the details, but as they spoke, she pictured him sitting in the flying bridge of *The Half-Moon* with the wind pressing his shirt against his body and the sun picking up the white of his teeth as he smiled.

"I'll be on the boat at five." He continued to talk, and she tuned him in. "If these men want to limit out on the big ones, we have to travel to the oil rigs. Tell them to get there on time."

"I'll make sure they know. Tomorrow afternoon I'll deliver weekly checks at the harbor. I should have the ones for tomorrow's charters with them also. What time do you usually get back to the dock?"

"I like to be back by four so we have time to clean the fish and give the customers time for pictures. You know, all the little necessities." He chuckled. "Why catch them if you don't have a picture to take home with you to brag about?" He winked at her as he pushed away from the desk. "Don't forget me. My boat's at your disposal."

Clear, blue skies, a gentle breeze, and almost nonexistent waves made the next day a perfect one for a charter. Russ was pleased. The four hotel guests didn't hesitate to show their excitement over the scenery and the fish. They even took turns playing with Hammerhead.

With the fish biting as soon as they dropped anchor at the oil rigs, they had no trouble reaching their limit on lemon fish.

The thrill of a catch still excited Russ even after all the years he had owned the boat. Today was no exception. Even though he had hired a young man as a deckhand, he liked getting involved with the fishing. The hiss of the line streaming out of the reel from the pull of a fish sent his blood racing. Sometimes it was all he could do to let the customers reel the big ones in.

He missed holding the pole and feeling the jerk of the fish at the other end of the line. Some days he even missed the soreness of the muscles in his body that came from a good struggle.

Today, his customers whooped and hollered and cheered one another as they pulled in fish after fish. He couldn't help but enjoy their excitement. It felt good to share his boat with men who appreciated it.

Sitting in the flying bridge alone on the way home, he let his mind wander at will. He had made his passengers comfortable below, and, as usual, he enjoyed these moments alone with the open water, the sky, and an occasional seagull flying overhead.

His thoughts turned to Nikki. She had always loved the water. He couldn't wait to find a day to take her out on the boat. He remembered times when the two couples broke away from their college campus and headed home to spend time on his dad's boat. With the worries of college courses left behind, they'd head for the islands.

He smiled, remembering how he and David used to watch Nikki and MaryAnn sunning on the bow of the boat. MaryAnn always kept her hat pulled down low to protect her skin, but Nikki held her face to the sun and let the wind take her hair.

Now that Nikki was back, he knew she'd appreciate being out on the water after being gone for so long. He'd have to make a point of taking her and Libby out for a day trip. It would do his daughter a world of good to share him with a friend. With her surgeries and recoveries, she'd become much too possessive of him—not that he was complaining. He loved spending time with his daughter.

He stretched his arms and tapped a few controls. Relaxing, he let his mind wander some more. He loved days like this. His thoughts floated with the gentle breeze, delighted in the warm sunlight, and skimmed along the foam on the water at the bow of the boat. The beauty surrounded him, sending a wave of joy through his soul.

In quiet moments like this he sometimes imagined a loving woman in the picture, usually a faceless presence. He'd long ago quit dreaming of his former wife, but he never forgot the feeling of real love. Sometimes his imaginings would include one of the women he'd taken out, but he'd quickly push those images aside. He dated occasionally, but no one had ever warranted a spot in his quiet time on the water.

As he looked out over the sparkling ripples, he knew

one day he might be able to share this life with someone special, but right now it was only a fleeting thought. He had quit reminding himself that MaryAnn had shattered their perfect marriage. He'd trusted her. It would be hard to put his faith in another woman.

He pushed the throttle forward, felt the power of the boat under him, then forced his mind to concentrate on what was real.

His reality was a boatload of tourists and a beautiful little girl waiting for him at home. Long ago he'd learned to concentrate on Libby and on fish and on boats—on anything to keep him from losing his mind.

Reality was sometimes cruel, but he'd learned there was always something to help you through it.

Tonight he'd hold Libby extra tight. That thought warmed his heart as he headed toward the mainland.

At the dock, the usual crowd of tourists gathered around to view the catch of the day. His four men posed with their fish for photographs and elaborated on their exploits. By five o'clock the deckhand had cleaned and packed the fish, and Russ loaded his four clients with their coolers onto the hotel shuttle.

With the boat cleaned and ready for the next days charter, Russ paid Joey his week's salary, then watched as the young man high stepped it down the pier. Russ chuckled, remembering when he too would have headed for a night on the town. Tonight he would be happy in his recliner in front of the TV with his daughter in his arms.

Alone he walked over to the faucet at the end of the pier, where he stretched to ease his sore muscles. Even though he had not reeled in the fish himself, he still ached. On days after an active charter, he felt the years catching up with him.

He removed his shirt, bent his head under the hose, and rinsed away the fish smell and the salt.

Nikki had one remaining check to deliver. She looked forward to seeing Russ. Maybe if his duties for the day were over, they could sit and relax and catch up on old times.

She stepped away from her last boat and turned toward *The Half-Moon*. She froze. With her heart in her throat, she watched Russ hosing down his body. He wore only a pair of worn denim shorts that clung to his well-toned waist and muscular legs. The water sprayed over his head and glistened as it ran down his deeply tanned arms.

It ought to be a crime for a man to look so good, especially when that man happened to be someone who was supposed to be like a brother to you. Not a good thing, she thought.

As Russ stood up and saw her, she waved. He grabbed a towel and ran it over his torso and his hair.

"Hi. Come on over." He pulled a shirt over his head, then motioned to the boat.

With his shirt in place, Nikki breathed a sigh of relief, not having to look at his bare chest.

He helped her board the boat.

Immediately the bottom half of the cabin door flew open, and Hammerhead lunged out. She reached down and rubbed his head. "Hey, boy. Did you go with the guys today?"

"Yeah, they said they wouldn't mind, so I took him."

"So, how was the trip?"

"Great! I don't think you'll hear any complaints from those guys. They had a ball." He continued to dry his hair. The movement forced the shirt open. Beads of water sparkled on the dark chest hair that peeked out.

Nikki swallowed hard and looked the other way. "I brought you your chest—*check*." Embarrassed, she bit her tongue. "It's what we agreed on, but if there were any extra expenses, we can certainly see to them."

Russ examined the amount on the check, nodded, and signed the receipt. He leaned over an ice chest. "Want a cola?" Not waiting for her to answer, he reached into the chest, then popped the top on two cans.

"Sit down and visit with me. We have a lot to catch up on."

He pointed to one of the deck chairs, then handed Nikki her cola. His smile reminded her how lucky she was to have a friend like Russ.

He pulled another chair next to hers. "Knowing you're in town and not seeing you is driving me crazy."

Nikki took a sip, then grinned. "If I remember right, your friend David used to call you 'crazy' when you wouldn't go along with some of those stupid schemes of his. He thought you had a screw loose for not wanting to follow him."

"Yeah, we always had different ideas about what was normal, but he was still my best friend back then. I guess you overlook a lot of flaws in your friends."

"And your boyfriends," she threw in. "I should've paid attention to all the clues he was dropping."

"Don't beat yourself up, Nikki. We were kids then. We saw the world through different eyes. Maybe I was a little crazy too."

"Not crazy, Russ. In fact, you were much more mature than the rest of us at the time."

Russ looked over the water, then back at her. "I had a lot riding on what I did. If I hadn't kept up my grades, my scholarships would've gone down the drain. I would've had to withdraw. The rest of you had parents who could pay. I didn't."

"And MaryAnn and I understood that. David didn't. She and I didn't have life handed to us on a silver platter, but we had it better than you."

Russ smiled, and this time the smile creased the lines around his eyes. "I thought I had it pretty good, just without the big bank account."

Nikki thought about Russ' close-knit family. "That you did. You had a lot more than the rest of us in the family department, that's for sure."

"Enough about my past. Tell me what you've been doing since you got back."

Nikki stretched her neck muscles. "For the most part

this job and moving into my condo hasn't left me much time to do anything else." She smiled. "And I'm loving every minute of it."

"That's great."

"Contentment. I feel it when I hit the bed at night and when I step around boxes in the morning. It's been a long time since I felt this way. It feels good, Russ. Really good."

"It's not easy to find that thing that makes us content. I'm so glad that you have."

"Who would've thought a job could be that thing?"

"Well, I think a lot of it is coming home, don't you?"

She nodded. "Definitely. Things look different, but it's still home. I found a great country-and-western station on the radio. I caught myself dancing around the condo the other morning while I was dressing."

"We'll have to remedy that situation." He grinned broadly. "Can't have a pretty thing like you dancing by yourself. We'll have to hit one of the lounges on the beach. There're some new ones. I don't get out much, but I've heard some of them cater to our tastes in music."

Nikki stood up. "Don't make idle promises. I plan to take you up on that suggestion. I haven't been dancing—really dancing—in years."

"Deal."

She changed the subject. "Would you like another charter? My boss gave me the names of some personal friends of his. They want a sunset cruise with a steak dinner Friday night. Are you free?"

"It's pretty short notice for a meal cruise, but I think I can swing it. I've got a morning charter that day, so I don't see where the scheduling would be a problem. The food might be a different matter. I'll call Mrs. Holmes. She can usually whip me up some side dishes pretty fast."

He talked about what he'd need to do, not so much to her as thinking out loud. She enjoyed listening to him. David had never done that in front of her. He'd kept his thoughts to himself, leaving her feeling left out of his plans. Left out of *their* plans. Their future.

The simple act of Russ' sharing his thoughts warmed her and lightened her mood.

"Go ahead and book me," he said as he stood up. "I'll talk to my sister to see if I can count on her to go with me. It'll take several hands to take care of a grill and run the boat too. I have an all-dayer tomorrow, but I'll call you when I get home."

With a smile hard to wipe off her face, she left Russ and Hammerhead on the back of the boat. When she reached the car, she turned. Russ was still watching her. For a split second their gazes met.

She waved, smiled, then waved again.

How great it was to be home. She pulled out of the parking lot. At the stoplight, she looked back. Russ had returned to his boat, probably unaware of how much his warm smile and friendship meant to her. Being back on the coast was wonderful, but having him here made it special.

She'd come home to restart her life and renew old friendships. She hadn't had much time to get reacquainted with her other friends—if any were left in the area. But that was okay. Finding contentment was a step in the right direction, and even if he didn't realize it, Russ was helping her find that missing piece of her life.

Chapter Three

"A barbecue? Sure. That sounds great!"

"This is just a spur-of-the-moment thing, nothing fancy." Russ' sister, Gayle, chattered in her usual up-beat way. "Mom wanted to see everyone together, so we're throwing some hamburgers onto the grill."

Nikki remembered the pleasant afternoons she'd spent with Russ' family long ago—so different from her own family's gatherings. Visions of her mother's picnics popped into her head—wrought-iron tables covered with linen cloths, brightly colored china, and huge vases of spring flowers. Not exactly a picnic.

At the beginning of her marriage she'd emulated the Preston family barbecues, but like every other good thing in the marriage, those were eliminated along the way and David's ideas of entertaining substituted. And as far as her mother's gatherings went, she never remembered having anything as mundane as hamburgers.

Gayle interrupted her reverie. "Do you think you can make it?"

"It sounds like fun. I'd love to come."

"Great. I've already told Russ about it, and I'm sure he'll call you."

Spending an afternoon with Russ and his family sent an unexpected warmth throughout her system. "I'll bring a cake or something sweet, unless you want me to make a salad or side dish."

"No, no, you don't need to bring anything."

"I insist. I'll bake a cake tonight, and I promise you, it won't be any trouble. In fact, I'd really enjoy doing it. I don't get the opportunity to bake much anymore now that I live alone, so this is a good excuse."

As soon as she hung up, Nikki dug through some of the boxes on her kitchen floor and found all the ingredients for her grandmother's chocolate cake recipe. Packing all those spices and staples had been a chore, but now she was glad she'd done it. Humming along with George Straight on the radio, she mixed, measured, and beat.

During her years of marriage to David, cooking was one of the things that kept her from feeling her life was completely useless. In the end, though, he managed to destroy even the joy she found in the kitchen.

As David's business grew, his preference for more frequent and more elaborate dinner parties became his way of standing out in the community. He bragged about her culinary abilities. In fact, he thought cooking was all she should do. Trying to convince him otherwise was useless. According to him, having a career outside the home was an unspeakable topic. Why would she want to work when he had plenty of money?

She sighed. *The man never understood anything about me.* It was always about him—him and the other women in his life, as she'd later found out.

She pushed that thought from her mind. Those days of trying to hold her marriage together were gone forever. The broken heart, the feelings of rejection, the questions—it was all behind her. Her life was now her own.

Looking up from the kitchen counter, she stared out the window. A boat raced along the channel just south of the beach, sending out a spray of water that sparkled like falling diamonds.

How calming, she thought. That's why she'd come back here. Moments like this would help her move on.

As she worked on the cake, she thought about Russ and his family. Then her thoughts settled on MaryAnn. MaryAnn should be joining them at Gayle's for the picnic as Russ' wife.

I hope you're happy with your new life, because there's a lot down here you're missing.

An unexpected wave of guilt swept over her as realized she'd be enjoying what her friend ought to be doing.

She shook her head. *That's stupid. Why should I feel*

guilty when MaryAnn chose to leave Russ and her daughter?

Still, the situation bothered her.

How long had it been since she and MaryAnn talked, really talked, like the friends they used to be? Nikki tried to remember. Had MaryAnn ever returned her phone calls after the divorce? No. MaryAnn had severed their friendship as if it were part of the divorce settlement.

She poured the cake batter into the pans. Thinking about what MaryAnn had done, Nikki shoved the pans into the oven, slammed the door, then leaned against it. Slapping her arms across her chest, she hissed. MaryAnn had ruined not only her own marriage but the life of her little girl and the beautiful friendship that they'd all had.

Nikki looked out the window at the calm waters. *You have no idea what you gave up when you left that man.*

Shortly after work the next day the doorbell rang, and Russ greeted her with a grin. "Hi. Am I too early?"

"No, not at all, but give me a minute. I'm ready. I made a cake."

"A cake?" He raised an eyebrow. "I'm impressed."

"Don't be. It wasn't that hard. But you don't have to look quite so surprised. What do you think I did all those years I was married? I happen to love cooking."

Russ followed her into the kitchen. "I'm not surprised that you can cook. I just didn't think you'd have the time to bake a cake."

Nikki gave him a friendly elbow in the side. "You got out of that one nicely."

Russ laughed, then helped out by carrying the cake to the truck. Juggling the dessert with one hand, he opened her door with the other. Hammerhead stood on the seat, taking up the entire cab of the truck.

Nikki warded off a big kiss as she slid onto the seat next to him. "Going to play with the kids, Hammerhead?"

"Oh, yeah. He loves going to Gayle's. But you might as well give him an ear scratch so he'll leave you alone."

Nikki did just that, then took the cake from Russ, glad that it sat safely inside its plastic carrier.

She laughed at his words, but in reality Russ could've said anything to evoke a smile from her. The twinkle in his eye and the dimple in his cheek when he smiled made her feel good.

She leaned against the leather seat and thought how lucky she'd been to listen to her heart and move home. What had taken her so long?

Gayle lived about twenty minutes away. Once they left the newly rebuilt commercial area along the beachfront, she marveled at the long stretch of beautiful sand beach. How she'd loved this area when she was a teenager. Today, brightly colored umbrellas dotted the sand, and groups of beachcombers and sunbathers took advantage of the summer sunshine, just as she and her friends had years ago.

They turned off the beach into a well-established

neighborhood. Large brick homes with manicured front lawns sat back along a tree-lined street. Flower beds that showed years of tending and the shade from the magnificent oaks in the yard added a pleasant, homey feeling.

"Just as nice as I remembered," she commented.

Russ pulled the truck in front of a redbrick house with dark green shutters and white trim. Immediately Hammerhead stood up on the seat, his tail slapping Nikki's arm.

Nikki laughed and leaned against her door to keep Hammerhead's tail from swatting her face. "I think he recognizes the place."

Russ opened the door. "Come on, pal, before you knock Nikki through the door."

As Russ slid off the seat, Hammerhead wasted no time in jumping out of the truck.

Russ leaned back into the cab. "I'm glad you came today. It's like old times."

As soon as the words passed his lips, he rolled his eyes, then slid out the door without waiting for a comment.

Nikki understood. Life would never be the same for him and his daughter, nor for herself. Even though visiting with Russ' family *was* like old times, little else remained the same.

By the time he opened her door, he'd plastered a smile onto his face, the awkward moment behind them.

Not waiting for them, Hammerhead raced through

thc open gate and around the house. Russ led Nikki up the concrete walkway lined with deep purple petunias and bright yellow marigolds, a few trampled down. The work of little feet, Nikki guessed. She hoped Hammerhead's gigantic paws wouldn't take out the rest.

After a quick knock on the front door, Russ opened it. "We're here, Gayle."

A muffled shout came from deep within the house.

Russ held the door open with his back. "Come on in. We'll find my sister in the kitchen."

As soon as they stepped inside, two little boys and a dark-haired girl darted from a hallway into the living room and headed for the front door, nearly knocking the cake out of Russ' hand.

"Whoa, kids!"

All three slammed into one another.

"Hi, Uncle Russ. Is this Miss Nikki? Is she your new wife?" asked the younger boy after coming to a screeching halt. Curly blond locks fell onto his forehead and over the tops of his ears. Big brown eyes looked her over. To Nikki he looked like a little angel.

"No, stupid. Miss Nikki's not his wife. I told you that. She's his girlfriend," explained the older one, who was probably seven at the most. He giggled as he looked from his Uncle Russ to Nikki.

Girlfriend? Wife?

Nikki stood stunned, unable to correct the child. The little girl, whom Nikki recognized as Libby, took a step back, her face pale and solemn.

Heat inched up Nikki's neck. She felt sure that, had she looked at Russ, his face would be as red as hers.

"Nikki, meet my two nephews, Mickey junior and Dougie. They'll put you straight on any subject you have a question about."

Nikki pulled her gaze up to Russ, whose eyes said he was sorry about the boys' outburst.

"Hi, boys. It's certainly nice to meet you two." She was about to say more, but both of them yelled "Bye!" and ran out the front door. Not sure whether to laugh or cry, Nikki looked at the closed door and said the only thing that came to mind. "They're precious!"

"Yeah, they are, but this big girl is the most precious." Russ shoved the cake into Nikki's hands, then reached down to pick up Libby. After a big hug, he gave her a kiss on the cheek.

Had there been any tension in Russ' face prior to picking up his daughter, it disappeared instantly. Joy and love radiated from the man's face.

"Daddy, where've you been?" Libby eyed Nikki from the corner of her eye, then buried her head under Russ' chin. "You're late."

"I've been at work. Didn't Aunt Gayle tell you I was picking up Miss Nikki after I cleaned the boat?"

Libby glanced at Nikki again, this time from over Russ' shoulder. "Yeah, I guess."

Russ put her back down onto the floor. "Aren't you going to say hello?"

The young girl, tall for her age with olive skin like

her mother's and big brown eyes like her dad's, stood before Nikki with a blank look on her face.

Nikki held out her right hand. "It's been a long time since I've seen you, Libby. You've grown up so much. You're beautiful."

For a moment Nikki thought the child would turn and run rather than acknowledge her presence. Finally, with an exhale of breath, Libby touched Nikki's hand, then withdrew hers quickly. Knowing she'd heard her cousin label her Russ' wife, then girlfriend, Nikki couldn't blame Libby.

She tried to speak in a normal voice. "I was a very good friend of your mother and your dad when we were young, and I've moved back home now. I remember you when you were just a little thing. You gave the best hugs."

Libby looked up to Russ. "May I go outside now?"

Nikki tried to hide the hurt generated by the girl's cool attitude.

Russ looked at Nikki again with another apologetic expression. "Sure. We'll see you in the backyard."

When the door slammed behind her, Russ raised an eyebrow. "You never know how kids will react, do you? I'm sorry she wasn't more welcoming, and, as for my nephews, what can I say?"

"Don't worry about it. They're children. They either say too much or nothing at all. None of them remembers me. I've been gone a long time."

Shaking his head, Russ nodded toward the kitchen.

"Come on. I'm sure Gayle could use our help, and you need to be reintroduced to the rest of the family."

Libby's coolness toward her spread uneasiness through Nikki. Russ was a dear friend. That's all he was. But she wondered if his family thought of them as something more.

Nikki inhaled deeply and followed. A large table in the middle of the room stood covered with chip bags, hamburger buns, covered dishes, and other assorted barbecue items. A tall woman with short brown hair stood at the sink washing lettuce. She turned as Russ and Nikki entered the room.

"Well, hi. Come on in." Gayle grabbed a dish towel and dried her hands. "Nikki, I'm so glad you could come. It's been much too long."

The sisterly hug from Gayle took away Nikki's misgivings about what the family thought of her.

Russ got hugged next. "Gayle hugs everybody," Russ said as he pulled away.

Gayle slapped him playfully with the towel. "No, I don't." She took the cake from Nikki. "Yum, this looks great."

"It's a recipe from my grandmother, and it usually turns out pretty good. I hope today's no exception."

"I'm sure it won't be. Why don't you two go outside? Mom and Mickey are out by the swing watching the grill. You know Mom. She thinks Mickey needs her help even after all these years. Maybe you can convince her to relax."

"Yeah, that'll be the day. Come on, Nikki. We'll carry some of this stuff out to the picnic table."

Nikki and Russ gathered as much as they could carry. As they stepped out the back door, Libby, little Mickey, Dougie, and several other neighborhood boys nearly knocked them down. Hammerhead lumbered close behind.

Nikki juggled a casserole dish and chips bag and laughed. "Whoa, boys. I think you'd rather eat this than wear it," she said. Some of them acknowledged her and laughed. The others, including Libby, kept running.

Russ pretended to grab at one of them as he flew by. Then he chuckled. "Man, to be young again and have that much energy."

"Were you and Gayle just as wild when you were little?"

"Yeah. It was great."

They loaded the food onto the picnic table, then strolled across the lawn to where Mrs. Preston sat on a swing suspended from the limb of a huge oak tree. She smiled and waved to Russ.

Russ sat down next to her, placed an arm around her shoulders, then planted a kiss on her cheek. "Mom, you remember Nikki Clark, don't you?" He patted the swing for Nikki to sit down next to him, but she didn't move.

Mrs. Preston extended a hand. "Of course I do. Glad you could get together with us this afternoon. Do you remember Mickey?"

Once the greetings were completed, Nikki squeezed in on the swing beside Mrs. Preston.

"Excuse me a minute," Mickey said, and he ran toward the front yard, where he yelled something to the boys.

Mrs. Preston spoke up. "He's got quite a crew of the neighbors' kids around here all the time, and he's so wonderful with them."

"I met the boys earlier. They're really cute." Nikki faced Mrs. Preston but could feel Russ' gaze on her. She hoped she wasn't blushing. All of a sudden this cookout didn't seem like such a good idea.

What was Russ thinking? Was he regretting having brought her to his family picnic?

"Those boys *are* cute," he agreed, not revealing any emotion about her being with his relatives, "but they've got more energy than I ever remember having. I'm not sure how my sister keeps up with them."

"You must have amnesia." Mrs. Preston rolled her eyes and exhaled loudly. "There was a time I'd cringe when I knew I had to take you and Gayle out in public. You two were terrible. Almost drove me crazy. You wonder why I'm as goofy as a goober now? Well, the answer is right in front of me, and those little boys are just following in the footsteps of their mother and uncle."

Russ laughed. "Let's hope not."

Mrs. Preston squeezed Russ' cheek. "Can't think of a better set of footsteps to walk in."

Looking embarrassed, Russ leaned back as his mother stood up. "Got to go help. You two enjoy the evening."

Nikki shifted and gave the swing a little push. "Maybe I ought to go help too."

She started to get up, but Russ placed a hand on her arm. Nikki's breath caught in her throat.

"Don't go. Sit with me. Mom and Gayle have it covered."

Even though she knew she should put some distance between Russ and her for Libby's sake, she didn't want to go.

"You sure?" she asked. "I'm not used to being waited on."

"Relax. You deserve a little pampering, and if Mom's not busy, she's miserable. Anyway, I haven't sat in this swing in years, and I'd like some company."

He grinned at her and speared her with a look that made her heart skip a beat. Finally he leaned against the back of the swing and looked up into the oak tree.

"Remember the big oak in my mother's yard?"

"Oh, yeah. That was the biggest tree I'd even seen. Is it still there?"

"Most of it is. We lost some of it in the last hurricane."

Nikki nodded, tilted her head up, and lost herself in the crisscrossed limbs and millions of leaves above her. "I remember sitting under that tree for hours with you and David and MaryAnn. Those were easy, carefree days, weren't they?"

"Yes, they were. The hardest decision we had to make back then was which movie we'd go see."

"Yeah, and the girls always lost. You two never took us to see what we wanted to see."

Russ chuckled, then talked about days gone by. Smooth and easy, his words washed over her as he recounted episodes from his childhood. Closing her eyes, she relaxed as the gentle back-and-forth motion of the swing eased the tension out of her body.

Nikki felt Russ' arm go around her shoulders.

"Are you asleep?" he asked softly.

Nikki pulled herself back into the present, but she didn't want to move. The weight of Russ's arm on her shoulders comforted her as she hadn't been in years. Involuntarily her body leaned into his. His was hard. Tense.

She opened her eyes and blinked. "Oh, Russ, I'm sorry." She sat up straight, and his arm slipped away. "I think I did doze off."

She looked around, embarrassed she'd been asleep but more because she'd awakened in Russ' arms. "I don't know when the last time was I've been this relaxed."

"I'll take that as a compliment." His gaze bore down on her.

For a moment Nikki held her breath. Russ was next to her, too close. When she heard the children's yells coming from around the house, she inched away from him until her back touched the arm of the swing. He did the same.

For a moment she felt like a junior high student at her first dance in the gymnasium.

She glanced toward the house, where Gayle, Mrs. Preston, and Mickey hovered around the grill and the picnic table. "I'd better make myself useful."

"Yeah. Me too." But Russ didn't move. He looked at her as if he wanted to say something. He didn't. Instead, he finally took her hand and helped her up. "Come on."

Together they left the swing, but she walked with her hands crossed in front of her body. She prayed that Russ' family and especially his daughter hadn't noticed the close contact. She and Russ hadn't done anything. Their closeness had been innocent—a quiet moment between friends—but for her it reached down deep within her soul and pulled up feelings she wasn't ready to deal with.

Embarrassed that she was probably reading too much into all of Russ' actions that evening, she pushed out a gush of air from her lungs and put a spring into her walk.

Grow up, Nikki. You're being ridiculous. Russ had done nothing but put his arm around her shoulders, a gesture common among any friends. Why had it startled her?

She walked up to the picnic table, where Gayle and Mrs. Preston prepared hamburgers for the children. No one indicated that anything unusual had happened on the swing, but Nikki couldn't push aside the awkward feeling.

Gayle moved over to let Nikki reach the table. She immediately grabbed a plate and began working on hamburgers for a half dozen little boys and one special little girl. The chore proved to be more fun than she'd ever thought possible.

Russ shoveled ice into cups as he joked with the boys running around him. Furtively he protected Libby from the roughhousing of her cousins. One after another the children lined up to vie for his attention. Russ teased them and easily took the physical abuse of the clowning seven-year-old boys.

Nikki admired Russ' little girl. She'd been through a lot. Not having a mother in the picture was horrible, but Nikki knew she'd also had to endure a series of operations on her legs, from the injuries caused in the wreck. So many nights she and Russ had talked on the phone, he in Libby's hospital room, she waiting for David to come home.

It had been a lonely time for both of them.

Today, though, there was nothing but smiles from Russ and Libby as the boys pushed and shoved to get their food first. Libby held her own with the little ruffians. Nothing about her indicated the hurt she'd been through. She even forgot to frown a time or two when she caught Nikki's eye.

Finally, with the children sitting at several smaller outdoor tables, the adults sat down to eat.

"Mind if I squeeze in?" Russ stepped over the picnic bench and slid next to her, his plate piled high with two hamburgers, a huge scoop of potato salad, and chips covering everything.

Nikki grinned.

"What?" he asked.

"Nothing. I'm glad you sat next to me. Now my plate doesn't look so full."

"My boy has never been shy about eating," Mrs. Preston observed. She sat on his other side. When she patted his cheek, Russ rolled his eyes. Everyone else laughed.

Mickey grabbed Gayle's hand, and everyone, including the neighborhood boys at the other tables, did the same as young Mickey rattled off the shortest and fastest thanks that Nikki had every heard. Everyone chuckled after the quick "Amen."

She looked up at Russ, who tilted his head and grinned. "Got to start them somewhere."

"He did great."

She reached for a fork, then settled back to listen to the disjointed conversations around her. Russ talked about his latest charters, answering his mother's endless questions. Mickey and Gayle took turns jumping up from the picnic bench to take care of one boy or the other. The children took turns tossing pieces of hamburger to Hammerhead.

No one seemed concerned by the commotion. Nikki's heart tightened at the show of affection among them all. It was a breath of fresh air compared to the formal flavor of her mother's backyard soirées.

Wooden picnic tables and benches never graced her yard. No children ran through the flowers. No screams or chaos of any kind resounded. Nothing but heavy, decorative lawn furniture covered with the newest, most fashionable fabrics would do for their well-behaved adult crowd and the one little girl in her pretty party dress.

Nikki rubbed a finger along the edge of her paper plate. Had there ever been a paper plate at her mother's? Never.

All of a sudden she realized how comfortable she was here among the extended Preston family.

"Anybody ready for dessert?" Gayle yelled over the other conversations, obviously loudly enough for the boys to hear.

"Me!"

"Me too!" shouted one boy after another as they raced toward the adult table, Libby in tow.

Russ stood up and brushed the grass from Libby's knees, then let her get in line with the boys.

After inhaling their slices of cake, the entire group of children rushed toward the front yard, dramatically lowering the decibel level.

Nikki moved toward Gayle's end of the table. "This has been a really great afternoon," she said as she helped to pass the cake around. "I haven't had this much fun since I stayed at my grandmother's house during the summers. I appreciate being invited to join in the fun this afternoon."

"You're welcome to come over anytime. I remember when all four of you were always around." Gayle's hand stopped in midair, her gaze moving to the ground. "I miss seeing Russ having a good time."

Nikki was stunned at the change in Gayle's demeanor. "I know these last few years have been hard on him."

"You can't begin to imagine." Gayle slid a piece of cake onto a paper plate and looked up at Nikki. "He's doing better. Now that Libby's on the mend, his life is getting back to normal. Or at least we hope it is."

Nikki reached for the slice of cake to take to Russ, but before she stepped away, Gayle touched her arm. "I'm glad you're here. Russ needs to get out more."

Nodding, Nikki turned and walked toward Russ, hoping she hadn't read too much into Gayle's words.

Chapter Four

Nikki's spirits soared. Sitting behind her desk on Friday morning, she reviewed her recent accomplishments. It had been a good week, both at the office and in her personal life. She had taken a big step by moving back home, and so far it had proven to be the right step.

She relaxed against the leather of her desk chair. Giving up her PR position in Chicago hadn't been easy. After the divorce she'd taken the first job offer that came her way, a position that proved to be exactly what she'd needed at the time. But even with the nice salary and friends she'd made in the company, she knew something was missing. She didn't feel at home anymore.

Coming back to the Mississippi coast was coming home in every sense of the word. Taking that first step in starting over hadn't been easy, but she'd done it.

She hadn't felt this good in a long, long time. She prayed that the feeling would last.

Right after lunch Russ called, and by the sound of his voice, she knew her week's perfect record was about to be shattered.

"Give it to me straight. What's up?" She put down her cup of hot tea.

"I hate to tell you this, but I've got some bad news."

"Uh-oh. Something happened with the cruise tonight, didn't it?" She stood up and paced the room. "I knew things were going too smoothly to last. Go ahead. I'm braced. Tell me."

"Yep, the bad news has to do with the cruise, but it isn't completely hopeless . . . yet."

Nikki sank back into her chair. "Don't beat around the bush, Russ. What happened to the cruise?"

"Gayle called me a little while ago to tell me she didn't think she could help me tonight. She took Dougie to the doctor. He's down with a fever and cough, and, of course, she doesn't want to leave him."

She remembered the little boy with the blond curls and big brown eyes and knew she wouldn't leave him alone either if she were his mother. "No, of course not. I wouldn't expect her to. I hope it's nothing too serious."

"No, the doctor didn't think it was, but she still feels uncomfortable leaving the boys when they're not well. Mickey is a good father, but she wants to be right there with her sons."

"I understand, but where does that leave the cruise?" She crossed her fingers and took a deep breath. This was the cruise that her boss, Mr. Melton himself, had personally asked her to arrange, and she had assured him that he had nothing to worry about. *Yeah, right.*

"For me to handle a meal cruise, I need an extra hand. I've called everyone I know who might be able to help, but at this late notice on a Friday night, everyone already has plans. Joey panicked when I asked him. Said he had a big date. Do you know anyone?" He cleared his throat. "Or, better yet, would you like to make a few extra bucks and come help me? That is, of course, if you don't have plans already."

Nikki held her breath, afraid to answer.

"Hey, you still there?"

"Yes, I'm here. I'm just thinking." Did he just ask her to go out on the boat with him? To be confined in close quarters with him all evening? Could she do it?

This was work. She was an intelligent adult. Of course she could do it.

"I'd love to help you out. And it really sounds like fun. But do you think I could handle it? I haven't been on a boat in a long time. I'd hate to get in the way."

"Sure, you can handle it. I remember those summers we'd sneak off from campus and spend most of the weekend on the boat. You were a born sailor. Anyway, I just need someone to serve a few snacks, help with the drinks and the meal while I'm driving, and maybe steer the boat while I work the grill."

"*Steer?* Obviously your memory is cloudy. I don't ever remember driving a boat."

His deep chuckle warmed her. "It's not that hard. We'll be going so slowly that anyone could keep it on course. After we get back to the harbor, you can help tidy up if you're not too tired. How's that sound?"

"I . . . I think it sounds like something I can do. Now, what do I wear, and when do I need to be down at the pier?" She didn't try to hide the smile that spread across her face.

"Then you'll do it?"

"Sure. Why not?" Of course, the whole time she was agreeing to go, she ignored the all-too-real problems that she knew her decision could cause. Could she handle being close to Russ all evening?

"Great! Wear long pants and sneakers, and bring a light jacket with you. Sometimes it gets a little nippy after the sun goes down. We need to leave by six so we can get in a good sunset for them. I hate to ask, but do you mind driving down to the harbor? I don't think I'll have time to pick you up, and I need you there at about five-thirty."

"Sure. How about Libby? Will she be coming along?"

"Not this time. She's made plans to sleep over at a friend's. It's probably better, since we'll have a boat-load of people."

"I was hoping I'd get to spend some time with her. I have a feeling she wasn't too taken with me at your sister's."

She heard Russ take a heavy breath. "Don't read too

much into her moods. I haven't figured out little girls myself. Moody one minute and bouncing high the next."

Nikki wasn't sure that what she sensed from Libby was merely a mood, but she'd chalk it up to that for the moment. "Okay, I'll pretend she really liked me, and we'll see how she reacts on our next visit. See you at the harbor."

She hung up and pretended not to feel the trembling in her body. Even though this would be strictly business, she looked forward to spending an evening with Russ and worried about what she'd wear.

The rest of the afternoon dragged. At twenty to five, she grabbed her purse, locked up the office, and rushed to her car. By the time she got to her condo, she was almost breathless with anticipation. She had to keep reminding herself that this was work as she threw things together for the evening's cruise.

Going through just about every piece of casual clothing she owned, she finally chose a pair of white slacks, a navy blouse, and a bright yellow belt. Putting on her white socks and sneakers made her feel very nautical, and as she looked in the mirror, she felt as giddy as a young girl getting ready for a big date.

She froze. She wasn't a young girl anymore, and this wasn't a date. This cruise was an extension of her job with the hotel, and, more important, she was simply helping out a friend.

Pushing out a big breath, she grabbed a white and navy Windbreaker and a baseball cap. "This is not a date," she mumbled again as she marched to her car. "Not a date. Not a date."

She used the short drive to the harbor to get into the right frame of mind for a night of work, but as she pulled into the parking lot and saw Russ lifting an ice chest from the back of his truck, her heart skipped a beat. This might be part of her job, but she knew she'd enjoy the night much more than she should.

"Hey, wait a minute!" she called out the window. "I'll give you a hand with that."

"I've got it, but thanks for the offer." He lowered the chest onto the pier, then turned to look at her. "I do this alone or with Joey just about every day of my life. I wouldn't know what to do with too much help."

Russ wore a crisp blue cambric shirt with jeans that clung to his hips and thighs. It was the first time she'd seen him in anything but shorts and a fishing shirt. Her breath caught a little in her throat.

"If you want to help, you can hand me some of those things from the pier after I get onto the boat." With three enormous steps he returned to the truck and lifted one remaining box.

"I can handle that." *But can I handle being around you?*

With one push Hammerhead bounded onto the pier, greeting Russ with a wagging tail that reverberated up to his ears. Russ put the box down, patted the dog's big head, and smiled at the black eyes that devoured him with love.

"He certainly loves you, Russ."

"Yep. He knows who feeds him, that's for sure."

"Oh, it's obviously more than that."

A wider smile was Russ' only reply before he and his dog jumped onto the boat.

After Russ unlocked the door, she handed the containers to him one at a time. "Is this the food?"

"Yep. Come on board, and I'll show you where it all goes."

Russ reached up to help her. His large hand, rough and scarred from his years on the boat, held hers securely. The brief contact reminded her that she liked the net of security she felt each time she was with Russ. Maybe that was a normal feeling with a friend. Then again, maybe it was something more.

Pushing that last thought away, Nikki stepped onto the boat. In the cabin she placed things where he pointed and tried to stay out of his way. Between stowing items and checking instruments inside, Russ even managed to step outside to light the grill and arrange the prewrapped potatoes.

Several times they touched arms or rubbed against each other as they worked to get the cabin ready. "Oops, you're going to fire me before this cruise starts if I don't stop running into you."

Russ stopped what he was doing for a second. "Not a chance. It's not often I get help as pretty as you on board. I'm used to looking at Joey or Hammerhead all day."

His friendly compliment, meant to put her at ease, did nothing but add to the confusion building in her chest. Nikki arranged the last of the supplies with her back toward him, hoping to hide her discomfort. This was going to be a really long night if she didn't get her mind straight.

"Anyway," he continued, "this cabin gets really small when there's more than one person trying to do something in here. You're doing just fine."

"Thanks, Russ. I'm trying." *In more ways than you can possibly imagine.*

When the hotel shuttle pulled up with their passengers, she was relieved to have other people on the boat with them.

"Come on, let's go welcome our guests."

Four men and two women hopped down from the van, laughing and joking with one another.

"Looks like we're in for a good time tonight," Nikki commented as they walked down the pier.

"Yeah. It makes for a pleasant evening when the guests are already in a good mood." He placed a hand on her elbow and escorted her to meet the group.

"I'm excited. I can't wait to get started." And she really was. This was what living on the coast was all about.

Russ winked at her. "Now, that's what I like to hear."

His unexpected wink made her nearly stumble, but with his hand still on her elbow, she caught herself and managed to put one foot in front of the other.

After the group settled down for the evening's entertainment, Russ took Nikki to the bow of the boat and reminded her how to remove the rope correctly and how to retie it when they returned.

"Just like riding a bike. It's all coming back to you, isn't it?"

"Yep. I guess I'm still an old sea girl inside."

"Good. I knew you'd remember who you really were and come back home to us one day."

Nikki looked up from the rope she held in her hand. His face was serious, too serious.

Instantly, though, his mouth turned up in a slight grin. "Nothing can take away who we really are, can it?"

Not knowing what to answer, she simply nodded and worked to coil the stiff rope on the deck. Finally, with a nod, Russ climbed to the flying bridge, leaving her alone to wonder about his words.

Did she really know who she was anymore? Could she ever find the true Nikki Clark after being smothered for so long in her former husband's world?

And, more important, was coming back to the coast the way to find that out?

Chapter Five

With the engines whirring and the generator quietly vibrating from somewhere below the deck, she heard Russ call down to her to remove the last rope.

Carefully she used the boat hook to remove the line from the piling and to pull it onto the deck. There she wrapped the rope into another neat curl.

"Good job!" he yelled to her when she finished.

She looked up and gave him a thumbs-up. He grinned, his solemn attitude from moments ago gone.

Her big smile was answered by another wink from him. Trying to hide the flush that rose in her cheeks, she waved, then turned her attention to the guests, who had made themselves comfortable in the chairs out on the back deck.

As Russ maneuvered the boat out of the harbor, she

served a tray of light snacks and drinks to the hotel guests. After making sure all their needs were met for the moment, she climbed onto the bridge with Russ.

"What do I do now? They're all served."

"Your next job is hard. You have to come sit by me and let me show you the sights along my coastline." He patted the empty space next to him on the double-seated bench. "Things have changed so much in the past years, you probably won't recognize the town from this viewpoint."

Having no alternative, she squeezed onto the small bench and pretended that sitting with his thigh touching hers *wouldn't* be the hardest job of the night.

"It's beautiful from here. I've missed the feeling of being on the water."

He nodded but kept his eyes on the busy channel's traffic. Although he remained alert to all that was around them, his cool, relaxed manner made her feel comfortable and safe, a feeling she remembered from the times the four of them had spent their summers on the water.

Sitting so close, she could feel the warmth of his thigh through the fabric of his slacks and the muscles in his arms tighten as he maneuvered the boat into the channel.

"This life becomes you," she observed.

He glanced over at her. "Yeah. I think so too."

"You made a good decision when you left your accounting business."

"I needed this, Nikki. I needed something to keep me busy, keep the money coming in, but something that gave me time to spend with Libby." He patted the steering wheel and grinned.

His gaze moved from side to side in the channel, watching the passing watercraft. Most were coming in from a day on the water and heading in the opposite direction. Russ and several of the boat captains waved and greeted one another as they passed. Not wanting to distract Russ from his responsibilities, she sat quietly and took in the sights.

To the south of the channel was the small, uninhabited island that she'd been to many times in her youth. From her vantage point on the boat, the vegetation and sand beach seemed to be just at arm's length from her. She watched a man in waist-deep water throwing a net to catch pop-eyed mullet. Using his teeth to hold part of the net, he gathered the lower section into his right hand and threw what appeared to be a perfect circle.

"Still catching Biloxi bacon," Russ said when he caught her watching the man.

"I love watching them cast their nets. I remember the strange looks I'd get in Chicago when I referred to Biloxi bacon. Sometimes I didn't explain that they were the fish that helped to keep the natives from starving during the Civil War and the Depression. I just let people wonder what kind of pigs we raised on the coast."

"Pigs, huh? Beaches and pigs don't really go together."

"I know. But it was fun watching people try to figure it out."

As *The Half-Moon* took a sharp turn to the south away from the mainland, the wide expanse of open water made Nikki feel small and awed. "This is as beautiful as I remember it to be," she said quietly.

He nodded. "No matter what we do, Mother Nature doesn't change much. She doesn't care if we're here to take in the view or not. She still puts on a show."

"My, aren't we poetic tonight?"

He chuckled as he settled back against the bench. He looked relaxed, in tune with his surroundings. "No, not poetic. Just being an old coast boy."

He glanced down at the lower deck. "I hate to disturb you, but before you get too relaxed, would you go down and check on our guests and turn the potatoes for me? When you get back up, I'll show you how to drive this thing. By that time it'll be my turn to go down to put the steaks on."

"I can handle the first part, but I don't know about the second." Her insides churned as she looked from the boat to the water and back again at the instrument panel.

"I have confidence in you. You can handle it."

She wasn't sure if she should be encouraged by his faith in her or if she should panic at his expectations. She decided driving a boat couldn't be much harder than driving a car, so she exhaled and nodded. "Aye, aye, captain."

Nikki joined the guests on deck, picked up their empty dishes, and refilled their glasses, then quickly hurried back to the bench in the flying bridge. She couldn't deny the enjoyment she was getting from Russ' quiet talking and pleasant manner.

"How are our guests?" he asked.

"They're doing just great. Mr. Havlin has appointed himself the official bartender, so I'm free of that duty for the time being. Hammerhead is sleeping at Mr. King's feet, and they both look quite content."

"Good. Now let's get you started." He pulled two levers back, and the engines slowed considerably. When the bow of the big boat leveled out, he stood up. "It's all yours. Slide over here."

Since they were only inches from each other, she couldn't see how she could get any closer, but she stood up anyway. He turned sideways and took his hand off the wheel.

"Now, take the wheel and drive it just like a car, but don't turn it too hard. It's very sensitive. Check the compass every so often, because right now you want to keep the boat heading a little to the east of due south."

She put both hands on the wheel and took a deep breath. He placed his left arm around her shoulders as he talked. "Steering isn't hard, but if you're uncomfortable with it, we'll just pull out of the channel for a few minutes while I get the steaks on."

Uncomfortable? He had no idea how uncomfortable she was with his arm around her.

"No, I'll do fine. It's just such a big boat, and we're up so high. This isn't the kind we used to go out on. I feel like I'm going to topple over." Actually she wanted to tell him that she felt comfortable and safe with him standing this close—if only he'd take away his arm.

"Don't forget to keep the boat in the channel. It's pretty deep out here, so there's a lot of leeway if you mess up, but you never know what might be beneath the water if you get too far out of the channel."

He pointed out the channel markers, then slid his arm away from her. She relaxed.

"You remember how to use the channel markers, don't you?"

She smiled broadly. "Yep. That I remember. How could I forget when you and David pounded it into our heads? When we're going out, keep the green markers to the right of the boat. On our return home, it's red on right."

"Great. I'll be back in a few minutes. I like to socialize a bit with the passengers, and I need to put the steaks onto the grill."

"I'll be fine. You'll hear me scream if I need you."

"You're right. It's not that far down. But please don't scare the passengers." He laughed as he eased between her and the seat to get by. As he did, Nikki felt the entire length of his body against her back. He acted as if it were no big deal, but to her it was excruciating. Her body went rigid. A flush stung her cheeks, but there was nothing she could do.

"I'm sorry. It does get a little tight up here." He reached over her and adjusted the controls again. "Call if you need me. I'll be right down there."

His big body eased into the ladder opening and slipped down it as if he were a slender teenager.

"Hi, how's it going down here?" His conversation with the passengers drifted up to her.

Nikki concentrated on her task. She could see the next channel marker because it was still daylight, but when she looked at the compass, she was west of due south. She tried to correct too sharply. The boat jerked. She looked down at Russ. "Sorry about that." He and the guests laughed.

Once she felt comfortable with the steering, she relaxed a little against the seat. Sitting on the flying bridge by herself, Nikki realized that even with the powerful boat under her, she had not been this relaxed since the Prestons' backyard cookout. The evening was serenity itself—quiet, peaceful, and almost hypnotic.

Fragmented bits of conversation floated up to her from the deck, but other than that she felt alone with the water and the sky and the occasional squawking of a seagull. She understood why Russ loved his job so much, and she pictured him here day after day doing what he did best.

As the sun dropped lower in the west, she hoped the passengers were noticing it. For the next fifteen minutes she watched the orb move toward the horizon, sending bright bands of orange, yellow, and red across the sky.

"How're you doing?" Russ broke the silence as he swung up onto the bridge and stepped next to her.

"This is great. It's going to be a beautiful sunset."

He came very close and took the wheel from her. "That's why I came up. I want you to take in every minute of it. It'll happen fast."

Sitting next to him, she felt him pull the levers again to put the boat into an idle. The sun seemed to move more quickly as it neared the horizon. When the bottom of the orange ball touched the edge of the horizon, she and the guests below oohed and aahed together.

"Oh, Russ. This is the most incredibly beautiful evening I've seen in years."

Looking pleased, he smiled. "I knew you'd like it. I remember when you and MaryAnn would make David and me stop whatever we were doing to watch the sun set. I get it now."

With a raised eyebrow, Nikki glanced at him. "You got it then. You just wouldn't admit it in front of David."

He laughed. "Yeah. Maybe you're right."

"Now that you own your own boat, you see this every day, don't you?"

"No, not really. I see the sunsets from this vantage point only when I have a night cruise. I see sunrises almost every day, though. They're almost as beautiful."

"You're a lucky man, Captain Preston, a really lucky man."

"Yes. I have to remind myself of that every so often, but I guess I am."

Nikki pulled her gaze away from the red-streaked sky and glanced at Russ. He wasn't looking at the sky either. He was gazing at her with an intensity that took away her breath.

He continued in his same soft-spoken manner. "There's a lot of beauty in this world, but sometimes we have to be reminded that it's there."

At that moment Nikki wanted more than anything to lean over and kiss Russ—not so much as someone in love but as someone who admires the other person. He'd been through so much, yet his attitude toward life was uplifting and beautiful.

Russ smiled at her and put his arm around her shoulders, pulling her against his body. Nikki relaxed against his arm and exhaled deeply. For the moment it felt right and natural to be there.

Nothing more was said as everyone on the boat watched the sun slowly disappear below the horizon, spilling its pink glow onto the water.

"I hate to spoil the moment," he said quietly. He placed a hand on her arm and squeezed lightly. "But I have to go check on my steaks." He got up, pushed the two levers to build up a little more speed, and left her alone again.

She steered almost in a trance. Since the divorce she'd worked hard at finding happiness and starting over. She knew she was on the right track in moving home, but it was Russ who seemed to have coped much better.

She admired him—but, then, she always had.

When the steaks were almost cooked, she and Russ traded places again. He had put up a table on the lower deck and had laid out everything she'd need to arrange the place settings. Afterward she stepped back and admired her work. The table could have rivaled those of any restaurant in the tropics, with its deep aqua cloth, bright yellow plates, and napkins with hand-painted birds. Apparently Russ had an eye for nice things. Of course, it might have been Gayle who had picked out the place settings, but for some reason she believed the choices had been his.

She served the meal, chatted with the group for a few minutes, then, grabbing two root beers, she went back up to the bridge to give the guests some privacy.

"Are they settled?" Russ asked.

She reclaimed her seat next to him. "Yeah, and the steaks really looked good. I know they'll enjoy them."

He pulled out a plastic container and opened it. "This isn't exactly steak, but it's hard to balance a plate up here. Mrs. Holmes usually fixes sandwiches for me so I won't starve." He offered the container to her.

"Oh, no. I don't want to eat your supper."

"You're not. I told her to fix enough for two tonight." He looked at her with his killer grin. "You don't think I can eat all this, do you?"

"I don't know. . . . I watched you eat at Gayle's."

"Well, I eat a lot, but not this much."

He passed the container of sandwiches to her.

"After I smelled those steaks cooking, my stomach is growling," she admitted, taking half a sandwich. "Ooh, this is good. Tastes like ham salad."

"Mrs. Holmes usually does it up right. She doesn't let me go hungry." He ate his sandwich in silence, watching the water ahead of him. "Do you cook a lot? Besides baking cakes, I mean."

She laughed. "Not a lot anymore. I used to like being in a kitchen, but since my divorce there's not much call to stand over a stove all day. I usually pick up takeout."

"That can get old. Libby and I know every fast-food place and even the nice restaurants in town. She may be little, but you ought to see her with the waitstaff. She knows exactly what she's supposed to do. Just like a little lady."

Nikki could tell it was hard for him to contain a smile when he talked about his daughter.

"MaryAnn got to be a pretty good cook." He stared straight ahead as he said it.

Surprised that he'd want to talk about his former wife, Nikki listened, hoping she'd get an inkling of what he was feeling about MaryAnn now or even a hint about why he thought she'd left.

"Even after working all day, she managed to get a well-balanced meal onto the table most nights."

"I'm not surprised. She might've been a beauty queen, but she and I used to talk about raising a family and doing the domestic thing. No, I'm not surprised that she was a good cook." Her gaze settled on the evening sky as she thought about the good times she'd had with MaryAnn.

He looked at her. "Sorry. I didn't mean to make you uncomfortable."

"I'm not uncomfortable. I was just remembering the things she and I did together. We had some good times. It just blows my mind that she could've changed so much."

"Yeah. We had some good times as well. I thought we were still having them—until she left."

"I'm sorry, Russ."

"Don't be. I'm over it." He looked at her. "Really. My only feelings toward her now have to do with Libby, and, well, you know how I feel about that."

He placed a hand on her thigh. "You have to find closure. It's like a death. Even in a divorce you have to find closure for yourself. I did, and this boat did it for me." He looked down at his hand, then pulled it back.

Nikki felt as though a part of her went with it. Was he embarrassed that he'd touched her? She prayed he wasn't. In the past there had never been embarrassment when he'd touched or held her in a friendly way.

"I'm glad for you. It's ironic, but I strived to make my marriage as good as yours was."

He laughed out loud. "Thanks for thinking that ours was so perfect. Personally I thought it was, but that goes to show you how much I know. Although, I'd swear that at the beginning MaryAnn thought so too."

"If only we could hang on to that newlywed love,

huh? I thought that's what David and I would always have."

Russ reached over and lifted her chin with one finger. "I know you and David had some major problems, but no marriage is perfect. We don't know what we're getting into when we walk down that aisle and give our lives to someone else. Sometimes it works, but all too often it doesn't. We both found that out, didn't we?"

"Unfortunately, yes."

Russ relaxed against the back of the bench. "Let's not talk about our failures." His voice lowered as he continued. "Like with everything else in life, time is a healer."

"I guess that's what I'm waiting for—time."

"Well, don't give up on it. I know you're trying to get your life back on track, and it'll get there. Don't give up. You're doing great."

"I am, huh?"

"Oh, yeah. Great." This time he faced her and smiled. "Eat your sandwich. You can't face the march of time on an empty stomach."

He looked over one shoulder at the group. "After you finish that, would you go check on them? If you're not helpful, you're not going to be left a tip."

"Oh, gosh, they'd better not stiff me. I'd be so embarrassed."

He grinned at her. "After dessert, if you want, you can scrape the plates and stack them. We'll wash them at the dock. It's a lot easier."

"Sure thing."

Glad to have something to do, she stayed with the group downstairs, talking with them and tidying the dinner mess at the same time. Before she knew it, she was stretching with the boat hook to loop the ropes of their vessel over the pilings at the dock. When she looked up to see if he needed her to do something else, Russ nodded and winked.

This time Nikki smiled and waved. She was getting used to Russ' winks and smiles.

When the hotel shuttle pulled away with the tourists, she and Russ walked back to the boat alone.

"I usually spend a good hour down here before I leave, cleaning up and getting ready for the next day's charter. I'd love some company."

He stopped abruptly. Had he actually meant to ask her to stay? Was he now regretting it?

She didn't give him a chance to change his mind. "I'd like that."

Her words seemed to ease his tension.

"Good." He placed a hand on her elbow and helped her on board. "Doing dishes doesn't seem so bad when you have company."

"Well, doing dishes happens to be my forte."

He laughed, but she got serious before they went into the cabin. "You can't imagine how much I enjoyed this evening. I appreciate being asked, so I'm glad to help if there's something you think I can do."

She didn't want the evening to end. Being on the water

had made her feel great, and, if she were honest with herself, she had to admit that being with Russ had made it even better.

He grinned. "Come on, Hammerhead. Let's get her into the galley before she changes her mind."

With his tiny sink filled with hot, soapy water, they stood side by side, taking turns dipping their dishes into the water and rinsing.

Russ talked as he washed. "No matter how late we come in, even when I'm down here alone, I love this part of the trip. It's peaceful, isn't it?"

With their hips touching and fingers connecting with each exchange of a dish, Nikki felt that peace. There was solace in the quiet of the cabin, and she was reminded how long it had been since she'd shared a quiet, private moment with a man.

The soft lapping of the water against the boat, the occasional distant screech of a gull, and the quiet snores from Hammerhead added to the serenity.

Evenings like this were meant to be shared by two people in love. She almost groaned when that thought popped into her head. She pushed it away and concentrated on getting the cabin back into order.

Together she and Russ replaced the dishes in their storage bins, each plate separated and shielded from the next with a cushioned mat. *Separated and shielded,* she thought. That's what she needed when she was in Russ' presence.

Leaving the tightness of the galley, she breathed easier. They finished straightening the cabin and back deck. Their talk was easy and natural, and she laughed at his corny humor. Being domestic and working alongside him felt right, a feeling that had been lost in her marriage with David.

"What else has to be done?" She reached to put away a magazine at the same time that Russ reached for it. Their hands collided. Each pulled back quickly, too quickly for a couple of co-workers. "Sorry," she said, and she folded her arms in front of her.

He tossed the magazine into a bin. "I need to go down below to close it up for the night."

"I don't guess I could go down there too. . . ." She knew she shouldn't have been so eager, but it was an innocent request, so she added, "I've never seen below decks of a boat as big as this one."

"The quarters are a little tight for you to follow, but you can stick your head in. You'll be able to see what's down there."

Outside, he opened the back hatch and squeezed his big body into a dim opening. She squatted down to peer into the hole. When he flipped on a light, she was amazed to see a whole new world under her feet. He pointed out two diesel engines, a large generator, and numerous other devices, such as pumps, a water heater, batteries, filters, and heaven knew what else.

It was too much to take in, but she listened to him explain it all to her. She liked watching him squeeze among the different devices. He pointed them out with pride, and even though most of what he said went over her head, she was attentive.

When he finished, he joined her on the back deck.

"I'm impressed," she said. "I had no idea all that was under our feet."

"It's quite a lot of stuff down there. It took me months to feel comfortable with it and years to understand it all enough to keep it running myself."

He turned out the lights in the cabin. "Before I go home, I usually have a cup of coffee at the restaurant. Would you like something?"

"No, I really ought to get home. Thank you again for letting me come along. I can't tell you how much I enjoyed taking a look into your new world."

"I'm the one who needs to thank you. You were marvelous with the guests, and your company was great. Maybe we can do it again sometime."

Her brain said, *Definitely not.*

Her heart didn't listen.

"I'd like that," she said out loud, then wondered where her sense had gone as she gathered her things to leave.

As usual, he helped her up onto the pier, keeping his hand on her waist longer than necessary. She willed herself to step away from him.

"Good night, Russ." Reluctantly she turned to go.

"I'll walk you to your car. You never know who you might encounter in the parking lot at this time of night."

She said nothing. How could she, with her heart in

her throat? He was protective and dear. She didn't want to leave him alone, but she knew she was doing the right thing by not staying.

The night air, heavy with midsummer humidity, warmed her skin as she raised her face to the sky. "I feel like I did when I was a little girl and my granddad would let me follow him to check the lines on his boat. I always thought my grandparents had a perfect world, living so close to the water. I guess now you live in that world too."

"Yeah, and now you're in it again as well."

His smile warmed her as much as the night air.

"Yes, I guess I am, now that I'm back home."

After unlocking the car door, she turned to him. It would have been so natural to reach up and kiss his lips and to run her fingers through his hair. Instead, she brushed that thought from her mind and blamed it on the lazy, Southern night that surrounded them.

He reached out, opened the car door, and placed a hand on hers. They looked into each other's eyes. Without a word spoken, she knew a moment like this in another time or another place would have demanded intimacy.

But tonight they both knew that a friendship stood between them.

Chapter Six

Yawning and stretching, Nikki opened her eyes to another Saturday morning on the coast.

Usually she hopped into her day with things she wanted to do, but today there was nothing pressing. After the evening she'd spent with Russ, a day off was a letdown.

Walking around the condo, she picked up a few scattered items. She reached for the mop to do the bathroom floor, frowned, and after just a few quick swipes, she hung it back in the closet. Mopping and cleaning bathroom fixtures wouldn't do it for her today. She had to get out in to the open air.

By midmorning she was driving down the beach highway, enjoying the view. Before she knew it, she was at the traffic light in front of the harbor. From the highway she could see *The Half-Moon* in its slip, but no one, not even Hammerhead, was on her deck.

Nikki wanted more than anything to turn into the harbor, but she knew she had no business at the docks this morning. No official business, that is. What would she tell Russ if he were there? When the light changed, she moved with the flow of traffic away from the harbor.

Without much thought she pulled into the hotel parking lot and headed for her office, but even before she unlocked her door, she knew she'd find a spotless desk ready for next week's projects. She shuffled a few things around. After reviewing her schedule for the upcoming week, she sat and tapped her fingers on her calendar.

She called a former co-worker but caught her walking out the door with her children. For a moment Nikki let herself imagine spending Saturday mornings at the ballpark with children of her own. At thirty-five she'd given up on ever having a baby, but it didn't keep the longings at bay. She bit her lower lip. Her shoulders slumped.

She'd told herself time and again that David's refusal to have children was a good thing now that the divorce was final. "Yeah, right." Her words echoed off the walls of her empty office.

Empty was how she felt anytime she let herself think about not ever having a family of her own.

But this day was too gorgeous to sit around moping.

She grabbed her purse. So far the only thing she'd done with this Saturday was waste time, but she could remedy that situation. She headed toward the hotel lobby to eat a light lunch before heading off shopping or sightseeing.

As she stepped into a short line at the pasta and salad shop, her heart raced. She spotted Russ and Libby ahead of her. She allowed herself a moment to watch the scene of father and daughter. Libby fidgeted, stepping onto one foot, then the other, and played with a piece of paper in her hand. Russ spoke with a man in front of him.

As if he sensed someone watching him, he turned toward her. The smile that formed on his face sent a tingle throughout Nikki's body.

She waved to the two of them.

With obvious good-byes said, Russ took Libby by the hand and stepped out of the line to meet her. "This is a nice surprise," he said as they approached. "What are you doing here? I thought you were off today."

"I am, but I had some free time, so I ran by the office to check on things." She left out the fact that she was bored to death.

"Well, I'm glad you came over. Join us for lunch."

Nikki looked down at Libby. "Would you mind sharing your dad during lunch?"

Libby shrugged—not exactly the invitation Nikki wanted. Of course, she'd watched her friends' children shrug too many times to jump to conclusions, but she had a feeling Libby would rather Nikki move on and leave her alone with her dad.

Libby looked up at Russ.

"This is Miss Nikki. Remember? You met her over at Aunt Gayle's picnic."

"I remember."

The flat statement with no emotion confirmed Nikki's suspicion: Libby wasn't thrilled to see her. Nikki pushed aside a wave of disappointment. "That was a great picnic, wasn't it?" Even though Libby would rather not have her join them, she thought it was important for MaryAnn's daughter to at least get to know her.

Libby only nodded. Getting onto the child's good side wasn't going to be easy. She looked up at Russ, who frowned down at his daughter. Afraid Russ would scold the girl, Nikki changed the subject. She didn't need to give Libby a concrete reason for not liking her. "How's Dougie?" She asked.

Russ raised his eyebrows to his daughter, then looked at Nikki. "Dougie's fine. When I dropped in on them this morning, he was running through the house as if nothing had happened."

"Good. I was worried about the little fellow."

They inched their way to the head of the line as they talked. The hostess, dressed in a sleek navy suit, greeted them with a smile. "Hi, Russ. Table for three today?"

Russ nodded. "Do you have something by a window?"

"Sure do. Follow me."

Nikki hesitated. "Maybe I should leave you two alone."

"Nonsense," Russ said. "We'd love for you to join us."

At the table Russ pulled out a chair for her, then one for Libby. With a few words of familiarity, the hostess left. A waitress immediately replaced her. Again her greeting told Nikki that Russ knew this woman as well. The waitress bent down and spoke softly to Libby, who smiled up at her.

Did Russ eat here often, or did he know the woman from outside the restaurant?

Nikki felt like a fifth wheel. Maybe Russ had come here today to see someone special.

Even though she would rather have darted out the door, she picked up her menu. It was obvious she'd ruined the lunch for Libby, but she hoped she hadn't ruined any plans for Russ as well.

Libby giggled out loud. Nikki looked across the table. The waitress was still bent low next to Libby. Libby's smile and obvious admiration for the waitress tugged at Nikki's heart. What she'd give for Libby to look at her that way.

The waitress finally stood up. "And, now, what'll you have, Libby?"

Libby answered the waitress without hesitation.

Russ nodded. "She definitely knows what she wants."

And what she doesn't want, Nikki thought, but she bit her tongue before the words completely ruined the lunch.

"She's quite a little lady and one of my favorite customers." The waitress took the rest of the orders, then sashayed across the room.

"I like her, Daddy."

Russ jerked his head around. "Uh, I do too. She's a nice lady."

"She's cool."

Nikki had a feeling Libby wasn't just throwing out innocent accolades for a friendly waitress. A few daggers aimed at her whizzed across the table in those few words.

Was she overreacting to the cold shoulder of a nine-year-old? The child didn't even know her. How could she dislike her?

Nikki listened to Russ talk with his daughter about something that had happened in school during the week. She and Russ commented at appropriate times, but mostly Libby talked.

"It seems as if you really enjoy school. Do you like to read?"

Libby nodded.

"I liked reading mysteries when I was in school."

Libby nodded. "I read them too. We go to the library. Miss Oglethorp always lets me and my friends check out books that aren't in our section."

"Well, then, she must know you're good readers. That's wonderful."

Libby rattled off the names of her girlfriends and the books they were reading. Her face glowed with excitement and animation as she talked about the group of children in one of the books who solved mysteries happening on a farm.

Every few minutes Russ nodded or threw in a few details from the book.

"Oh, yeah. I forgot that," Libby would say, then zoom off with the rest of the story.

It was obvious that Russ had read every one of the books with his daughter. Nikki's heart swelled.

Watching Russ with Libby and being with him again lifted Nikki's spirits. Even though she knew she was treading on dangerous emotional grounds, she couldn't wipe the smile from her face.

They finished their meal at about the same time that three of the farm mysteries were solved. Nikki considered Russ' situation. At first she'd thought how lonely it must be to eat with just his daughter every day, but now she realized that Russ really was a lucky man. He might not have a wife any longer, but he had something in Libby that was priceless.

After the main course Nikki followed Russ and Libby to the ice cream bar, and then the three of them walked out into the lobby.

"What are you doing this afternoon?" Russ wiped away a glob of chocolate syrup from Libby's blouse, then looked up at Nikki.

"I don't know. There are a few little shops downtown I'd like to browse through, but I really haven't made up my mind."

"Libby and I we are going to a movie to relax a little before my cruise tonight. Want to join us?"

Nikki glanced down at Libby, whose mouth stretched into a grimace. That's all it took to know that the girl had shared her dad long enough. "I'd love to go, but I have some other things to do today when I get home." A little white lie would be better than adding to Libby's dislike of her.

"Well, I guess Libby and I will have to take care of all that popcorn by ourselves, even though we'd enjoy your company."

She was glad when he accepted her excuse and didn't ask her to elaborate on the lie. Maybe he understood his daughter's feelings, or maybe he was just being polite when he'd asked her to join them.

That last thought hurt.

"I'd better go. Thanks for treating a starving lady to lunch."

"Believe me, it was my treat." They headed toward the elevator. "You in the parking garage?"

She nodded.

"Me too."

They waited together for the elevator door to open. The silence was awkward. Libby stepped between Nikki and Russ and clung to Russ' hand.

Again it was hard for Nikki to ignore the belt of disappointment that hit her.

The three of them stood side by side in the small

elevator. The silence became unbearable. Finally the elevator door opened onto their floor. She breathed a sigh of relief.

Out in the safety of the parking garage, she surprised herself by touching Russ' arm. "I want to tell you again how much I enjoyed being on the boat last night. It was the most pleasant evening I've had in a long time."

"I'm glad you enjoyed it. The invitation remains open anytime you'd like to join me. I thought we made a great team."

Libby's audible exhale of breath reminded Nikki not to elaborate too much on the time she'd spent with Russ.

"I'd really love to do it again." She pointed ahead of her. "That's my car."

Russ took Libby's hand, and together they walked through the covered garage, an obvious wall of tension separating Libby and her. More than anything she'd love to have Libby take her hand as well, but she knew enough about children not to push the issue.

If she were going to renew her friendship with Russ, Nikki knew she'd have to do a better job with Libby.

Russ held Libby's hand and watched Nikki drive off.

Most pleasant evening? Was that how she felt about being with him on the boat last night? Those were her words, but *pleasant* in no way described his reaction to being with her.

Dynamic.

Breathtaking.

Mind-boggling. Anything but *pleasant*!

He shook his head, silently berating himself for letting his feelings go haywire for someone who should've been like a sister to him.

He had to stop acting like Joey or one of the other young guys who worked as deckhands for him and start acting more like an adult with a little intelligence. He looked down at Libby, who glared at Nikki's car leaving the parking garage. He reminded himself that he was a grown-up with a lot of responsibility and a little girl who needed him.

As much as he wanted to include Nikki in his life once again, he knew he'd have to tread carefully. Being with Nikki had made him remember how lonely he'd been for the last five years. He'd tried dating. He went out with the daughters or nieces of every one of his mother's friends. He took out a few women he'd met through charters.

The dates were fine, but after one or two evenings with the women, he decided he'd rather spend his time after work with Libby.

Was it Nikki, or was she simply someone making him realize he was ready to enter the world of the living again?

"Come on, Daddy." Libby pulled at his arm as she marched across the parking garage.

Russ knew that if he let his feelings grow, someone could get hurt.

Libby wasn't ready to allow anyone else into their lives right now. Did he have the right to force Nikki on her? He knew the answer to that. Eventually there might be someone in his life again, but how would he know when it was time to let that someone in?

He'd told Nikki that time was a healer. That's the way it would have to be with his daughter. Time would take care of her attitude toward Nikki. No way could Libby be around Nikki and not fall in love with her.

He wondered if anyone could. Even him.

Chapter Seven

Nikki hung up the phone, looked at her calendar, and smiled. Unbelievable. Amazing.

From the first week in July the charter business had taken off faster than she imagined it ever could. Scheduling trips, arranging transportation, keeping up with the expenses—all of it kept Nikki's life in a whirlwind.

She relished the feeling of contentment. Everything was falling into place for her—that is, except her social life. She attributed the nonexistence of dating to her busy schedule and being new to the coast.

At least that's what she kept telling herself.

She talked to Russ on the phone several times each week and saw him at least once a week at the docks. Each time she met him, she tried to be all business, but her insides told her she was fooling herself. He was friendly but not like before. She wondered if something had happened. Knowing a strictly business relationship was for the best, she left well enough alone.

As the summer advanced, so did Russ' tan. His body looked harder and leaner in his shorts, making it more difficult to keep her eyes off him when she delivered his checks. Rarely did he have a shirt on in the afternoons as he cleaned the boat after a day on the water. Several times he saw her coming and grabbed a shirt before greeting her, but sometimes she was at the boat before he realized she was there.

On those days she allowed herself the privilege of watching him spray down the boat or work on a reel or something as simple as moving an ice chest off the boat. She loved the intense dedication he put into his job, and she hated herself for wanting to spend more time with him.

Today, as she headed toward the boat dock, she found him cleaning a large fish for one of his passengers, who gathered around the table to watch. As usual, most of the women clicked pictures of him.

One woman in particular tossed her blond hair back, smiled at him, and leaned very close with her camera. Russ looked up and smiled as the woman requested. Nikki wanted to yank the camera from the woman's hand, since Russ was obviously enjoying her attention. Memories of seeing David react to other women came back to Nikki.

She clutched her paperwork a little tighter and swallowed the hurt. Angry at herself for allowing thoughts of David to ruin her afternoon, she headed toward the group of tourists.

Russ skillfully whipped his fillet knife through one side of the fish, flipped it over, and sliced through the other side. After rinsing two perfectly cut fillets, he placed them carefully into a traveling container. The woman smiled and leaned forward for another picture.

Russ smiled again, but as Nikki got closer, she realized his smile wasn't genuine. In fact, he looked exhausted as he pulled the skin from the next fish.

She wanted to rub his sore arms and massage his back. With her fingers she could soothe away the tension in his forehead, but first, of course, she'd have to get past the blond.

At that moment Russ looked up and saw her. "Nikki, I didn't see you standing there. Come on over." He continued to clean the fish but managed to give her a big smile, one that couldn't have been more sincere.

The woman's gaze slid from Russ to Nikki; then she slipped her camera back into its case.

"When did you get down here?" Russ continued to work the fillet knife but spoke directly to her.

"Long enough to be impressed with the way you wield that blade." Her cheeks burned from embarrassment, even though there was no way he could possibly know the momentary jealousy she'd let run wild.

He motioned with his head for her to come closer to him. "Just trying to get finished today." He spoke softly for only her to hear. "It's been a long week, and I'm dead tired. I've had a charter every day this week and still managed to get in two night cruises." He straightened his back and twisted to stretch. "I'm not complaining, but the old body's starting to feel the strain."

"Have you considered hiring another deckhand?"

"As a matter of fact, I have word out now. I've been looking, but at this time of the year it's hard to keep the old deckhands, much less find new ones or additional ones. Know anyone who might be interested?"

"I'd volunteer, but I don't think my knowledge of fishing would land the job—or the fish, for that matter—but I hope you find someone soon. You look like you could use some help."

"Oh, I'll get through it. Don't worry, and don't cut me off your charter list." He laughed and turned to finish packing the fish. "Got to make the banknotes on this girl."

It was the closest thing to a conversation they'd had since their lunch in the hotel.

Nikki brushed a stray strand of hair from her forehead and stared out at the open water. She thought she had figured out her position with Russ, but the more she saw him, the more confused she became. She wondered how long this strictly business arrangement would last.

More tourists gathered around them to take in the day's catch.

"You look pretty busy," Nikki said. "I'll put your check in the cabin and see you later."

"Sorry I'm tied up. I'll call you."

She nodded as she turned to walk down the pier to the boat.

Would there ever be a time that would feel right to try to get closer to him? For the moment she wouldn't let herself even consider the fact that something could possibly develop from their friendship. In her heart she knew it's what she'd love to happen, but it was obvious that Russ wasn't aware of how she felt.

She'd said that Russ had been the smart one of the group. Maybe he still was. Maybe he knew that trying anything beyond what they had could ruin a beautiful friendship.

Waving to Russ on her way back to her car, she tried to convince herself that she was opting for a horrible hurt if she let her feelings get out of control.

No, Russ was her friend, and that's how their relationship would stay. She would have to be content to be back home and enjoy the times she had with Russ and Libby.

By the middle of August Nikki found herself glued to the TV when the Gulf Coast found itself under its first storm advisory. Bertram, the second named storm of the season, had entered the warm waters of the Gulf of Mexico and was headed in their direction.

Lucky us, Nikki thought, and she tried to make herself laugh, but she knew it was no laughing matter. After only a few months in the area, she wasn't ready to face a storm, much less a hurricane, if it came to that.

The hotel handed out a list of hurricane preparations.

Even though she remembered her parents getting ready for storms, she still studied the list carefully. After making her own shopping list, she stopped in at the local grocery store on the way home. Her quick stop turned out to be a test of endurance. Hordes of shoppers jammed the aisles of the store, all grabbing the same items off the shelves: batteries, candles, water, and canned foods that she'd never eaten before.

Obviously everyone had a list.

Bertram reached hurricane status by the second day, and Nikki responded just as quickly. It wasn't predicted to be a bad hurricane, but remembering the beachfront after previous hurricanes, she didn't think twice about wanting to evacuate. With an unsteady hand she picked up the telephone and made a reservation at a hotel about eighty miles north of the coast, just as one of her co-workers had suggested.

Placing the receiver down, she sat at her desk and listened to the sound of her own breathing in the quiet office. She watched people through her office window going about their usual business, and she wondered why they weren't as worried as she was about this storm.

By late afternoon the coast was officially put under a hurricane warning. Following the hotel's instructions, she worked to secure everything in her office. Nikki tried to move quickly, but her actions were jerky and awkward. Twice she dropped stacks of papers and had to kneel down to gather them up.

As she crawled around the floor gathering her papers, she thought about Russ. What would he do with his boat? Would anyone help him?

She didn't have to think about his situation long. The door flew open, and Russ stepped in. "Russ, what are you doing here?"

"And what are you doing on the floor?"

"Just a little clumsy today, I guess."

Russ stooped down and picked up the remaining papers, then helped her to her feet.

"Thanks, but why are you here? Shouldn't you be moving your boat around to the bayous like everyone else?"

"I'm on my way to the harbor right now. I wanted to stop in here first. I was worried about you." Placing his hands on the back of the chair in front of her desk, he stood rigidly.

"I booked a room in Hattiesburg."

"Nikki, there's a lot more people on the coast than when you lived down here before. Do you know how hard it is to get out when three counties evacuate? You shouldn't be by yourself."

His concern some how eased her worry. Nikki relaxed against her desk chair and watched his grip on the chair back loosen. Blood flowed pink into his knuckles again.

"Libby and I are going to stay with Mom. She doesn't want to leave town in a storm this small, and I can't let her stay alone. Why don't you join us? She'd love to have some adult female companionship."

"I don't know. . . ."

How would she handle being confined again with Russ? But even as she worried about his closeness during a long night, her fear of facing disaster alone won.

"I guess I could. Anyway, it would be a relief for me to be with you and your mom. I am a little nervous."

"Don't apologize for being scared." He smiled and released the chair back. "I have to take my boat up into the bayou, and when I get back, I'll pick you up at your place. Take along anything you want. Park your car in the center part of the parking garage across the street. I think it'll be as safe there as it would be anywhere."

"Russ, are you sure your mom won't mind if I spend the night with your family?"

He looked shocked at her question. "Certainly not. She raised us better than to let a lady spend a night alone during a storm." He took a step toward the door. "See you when I get back."

Relief, gratitude, and a deep feeling of something that she dared not name washed over her. After rushing through the last two days worrying about her first hurricane in a long, long time, it was a pleasure to sit down for a few minutes to absorb the calm that Russ had just given her.

Gathering her purse and a few other personal possessions, she left the office.

By six o'clock she paced her living room, a small suitcase waiting by the door. She stared out the front window in amazement at the bumper-to-bumper traffic heading toward the interstate. Glad to know she wouldn't be in the parade of cars heading north, she smiled as she canceled her hotel reservation and made herself a cup of hot tea.

Seated by a back window, she watched the dark clouds roll low across the sky, nearly touching the rising swells of water. The wind whistled around her building. She shuddered as a chill traveled through her.

The normally serene water of the Mississippi Sound that had soothed her body and mind since she arrived now crashed against the piers, spraying the remaining parked cars and boats. The warm tea did nothing to stop the queasiness she fought to control as she thought about what was to come.

The sound of the doorbell jerked her back to the present.

"Hi," she said to Russ when she opened the door. Relief once again rushed through her at the sight of him. He was wearing a short blue rain slicker over a pair of jeans and a T-shirt. The rain made his hair look curlier and darker than usual, and in spite of the fact that his face showed the strain of the day, he greeted her with a big smile.

"I'm glad you're here," she said.

"Me too. Things are getting pretty bad out there. I don't know what's worse, the weather or the people trying to get away from it. Do you have a raincoat?"

She grabbed an all-weather coat from the back of a chair. "Right here. I think I have everything but the kitchen sink in this suitcase."

"Do you want to take your TV or any other valu-ables? Mother always takes her photo albums and sen-timental pieces of jewelry when we have to leave. I don't think the storm will get that bad, but you never know. It's always best to be on the safe side."

"I stuck a few things like that into the suitcase. I'd like to keep the TV safe, but it seems like a lot of trou-ble for you."

"No trouble." He walked over, unplugged it, released the cable, and picked it up.

As he juggled the TV to get out the door, she wanted to reach out and hug him. Never had she been so com-forted by anyone's presence.

Hammerhead sat up tall and straight on the seat of the truck. Nikki knew the minute he spotted them. His ears perked up, and he stood up, pushing his wet nose against the driver's window.

"Hey, boy. Remember me?" Nikki said to him as she slowly opened the door. Hammerhead nuzzled her hand. "I think he remembers me, Russ. Look."

"He's got a memory like an elephant. He never for-gets a good ear scratcher."

She slid onto her seat, and after Hammerhead gave Russ a wet lick across his arm, the dog sniffed her, then settled down by her side.

"He loves to be in the truck. We may not be able to get him out of it at Mom's if this is where he decides to ride out the storm." Russ looked around the dog at Nikki. "Ready?"

"Sure thing. I don't want to face this storm in a beach-front condo or in its parking lot, so let's go."

With more patience than Nikki thought she would have, Russ inched his truck into the lines of traffic on the highway amid honking horns and a couple of fists shaking in the air.

"I forgot how hectic it could get before a hurricane. I can't believe how panicky everyone looks."

"There're a lot more people living down here than when you were here before," Russ reminded her. "Lots of newcomers. Tempers run high when everyone starts trying to leave at the same time, especially for the first storm of the season. I think they remember the last big one."

"But this one isn't supposed to be too bad, right?"

He dragged his gaze away from the traffic for a second and flashed her a smile. "Right. Don't worry. We're fine."

He braked abruptly as a car pulled into the flow of traffic. With a long exhale of breath, he shook his head. "Thank goodness all this will be over fast and everyone will be safely where they're going soon. Everything will be okay, especially if this storm changes course and heads somewhere else." He chuckled before continuing. "Then everyone will gripe that all the trouble was for nothing."

"You think it might not hit here?"

"The last three times we've been under a hurricane watch, the storms changed course."

"I wouldn't mind missing this experience. I'm not looking forward to it at all."

"It'll be okay, I'm sure . . . I guess, I hope . . ." he joked with her.

"Don't you laugh at me because I'm as scared as most of the people in the cars out here."

"At least they're leaving. We'll leave, too, if the winds are predicted to go over one twenty-five or so. Of course, you have to leave before it's too late." He kept his eyes on the road as he talked. "Mom's house is pretty sturdy and set high. It's protected us all these years, so don't worry."

He patted her knee.

Why did she feel so reassured? He was just a man, but then, she knew he would do everything in his power to keep her safe.

The usual fifteen-minute ride to his mother's took forty-five, even with his using back roads and side streets, but finally they turned into his mom's driveway. The flower beds in front of the porch were newly weeded and spilling over with red and yellow blooms. "This is so pleasant. Do you think it will look like this tomorrow?"

"Hope so. If we're lucky, Hammerhead will do more damage to her flowers than the winds will."

As if knowing he was the topic of conversation, Hammerhead stood up on the seat. Nikki ducked as his tail knocked against her and anything else in its way.

Russ opened his door, and the dog lumbered over him, then jumped to the ground.

"Guess he decided to spend the storm with us instead of in the truck. Come on, let's join him."

Mrs. Preston met them at the door with outstretched arms, Libby coming up close behind. "Daddy, did you put the boat up?"

"Yep. The boat's all 'up' and safe in the bayou."

His mother wore a neat pink slacks outfit and fluffy house slippers. "Hi, son." She kissed him on the cheek. "And, Nikki, we're glad to have you here with us."

"Thank you, Mrs. Preston. I hope I'm not imposing."

"Heavens, no, honey. No one should ride out a storm alone." She turned to go in, taking Libby's hand. "Get your things inside, because I'm sure Russ will need you to give him a hand around here. I started, but I didn't get very far."

Russ and Nikki carried their belongings from the truck. After taking a moment for hugs and kisses with Libby, Russ headed out to the yard to finish the job of securing objects that might be blown around.

Mrs. Preston stood at the screen door. "Libby and I moved a lot into the shed already, but I just couldn't get all this stuff. I swear, every year it looks like I accumulate twice the junk I had as the year before."

The bond between Russ and his mother was obvious. What a nice change from the much too formal relationship David had with his family, or, for that matter, her relationship with her own. How she longed for what Russ had.

Nikki helped Russ take down Mrs. Preston's porch

swing, turned heavy chairs upside down, and moved trash cans and flowerpots into the shed. Russ stayed by her side, refusing to let her lift too much or get too far from his sight. The weather deteriorated by the minute, but Russ' presence made her feel warm and safe.

By the time they secured the yard, the sky had darkened, and rain came down in intermittent bursts, reminding Nikki of waves moving onto the coastline. Trees swayed gracefully with the gusts of wind, but she knew those same trees could inflict severe damage if they were uprooted or broken by high winds.

Russ put his arm around Nikki's shoulders as they came through the door. His casual motion sent warm sensation throughout her body, even though his slicker was cold and wet.

He grinned. "You look like a drowned rat. We'd better get you dried off."

"You don't look too good yourself," she said, but it was a lie. He wore the effects of the weather like another suit of clothes, a natural part of his being. The rain slicker, the wet hair, the drops of water dripping down his face—nothing could have made him look any handsomer.

They both emerged from different bathrooms wearing long, drawstring pants and soft pullover shirts.

"I'm glad you brought something comfortable," he said. "These nights get awfully long. If you'll give me your wet clothes, I'll throw them into the washer with mine." He started to take them from her.

"I can handle this chore if you'll tell me where the laundry room is."

"If you insist. Follow me."

He carried his wet jeans and shirt into a cozy little room off the kitchen. As they deposited their load into Mrs. Preston's older-model washer, she thought how proficient he was at domestic chores. Taking care of his daughter alone had made him become both mother and father.

Before she could get too mellow, he shut the lid. "If we're lucky, they'll be washed and dried before the electricity goes out."

"Thanks. You do good work, Captain Preston."

"Just call me Captain Mom. I'm not real good at ironing those little girl dresses, but I'm a whiz in the laundry room."

He straightened up and stretched. Then, with his hand at the small of her back, he led her into the kitchen.

Libby sat at the table, totally absorbed in a game on a small laptop computer until Mrs. Preston placed a cup of hot chocolate in front of her, filled to the brim with melting marshmallows. Libby wasted no time in taking a big sip.

Russ bent down and kissed his daughter on the cheek. She looked up at him with a frothy smile. With no apparent conscious thought, Russ picked up a napkin and wiped her lips clean. "Granny said you helped her pick things up around the yard."

"Yep. We worked hard moving all that stuff."

"I'm proud of you for helping. Thanks. It made Nikki's and my job a lot easier." He patted her on the back, then sat down.

Nikki pulled out a chair across from Libby and thought how nice it was to be among a family again.

Mrs. Preston leaned over the table and filled three cups with steaming coffee. "This is going to be a long night, honey. Enjoy the coffee before the electricity goes off."

Nikki placed both hands around the warm cup. "Thank you. This is wonderful."

Russ looked up at Nikki. "This is exactly what we need. I'm afraid Mom's right. This will probably be a pretty long night."

Hammerhead made himself at home on a rug next to the refrigerator, seemingly oblivious to the bad weather brewing around them. She wished she could be so calm. It had been a long time since she sat through a hurricane. But then, she wondered if that was the only reason she felt a little on edge.

Russ took a couple of sips, then stood up. He checked the supply of candles and two kerosene lanterns, then put new batteries into the radio and several flashlights.

Was Russ as nervous as she was? Maybe *nervous* wasn't the right way of describing what she felt. Why would she be nervous being with her friend and his family? But then, she only had to look at Russ to realize maybe *friendship* wasn't the right word either.

Russ and Mrs. Preston were both right. It was going to be a long night.

She focused her attention on the small kitchen TV tuned to the weather station. "The storm is located at latitude 29, longitude 88.5."

Mrs. Preston wrote down the coordinates, then added another dot on a well-worn tracking chart as the announcer continued.

"Bertram is only a Category One at the moment with the minimal seventy-five miles-per-hour winds but is expected to reach the ninety-six miles-per-hour winds to become a Category Two or possibly a Three by landfall in the early-morning hours. It's a widespread storm, and the lighter bands of wind and rain are already starting to be felt in the coastal areas of Mississippi and Alabama . . ."

Nikki took it all in as she sat in silence. This was a scene well known to those who lived along the coastlines. How well she remembered. She looked at Mrs. Preston. "How many hurricanes have you ridden out in this house?"

Russ and his mom looked at each other as if they'd never really thought about it before.

Mrs. Preston answered. "One to three warnings that make you go through all the preparation isn't unusual for a year, but it's rare that a storm hits us directly. What do you think, Russ? Do you suppose we've been through about six meaningful ones in your lifetime?"

He nodded. "If that many. It's like Mom says. We make more preparations than needed, but you never know where the storms will actually make landfall. You have to prepare, though."

Mrs. Preston nodded her agreement. "Nikki, how long did your family live here? Surely we had a few storms while you were here, didn't we?"

Nikki thought a moment. "Yes, ma'am, but just a couple. My father was transferred here with the military at the end of my ninth-grade year. I called this home until I married, so I guess that adds up to about seven or eight years. I remember we prepared for a couple of storms while I was in high school, but none was very memorable."

"Nothing wrong with a wimpy hurricane," Mrs. Preston said as she looked over her chart. "When it comes to storms and hurricanes, I'll take nonmemorable ones any day."

"In reality," Nikki added, "about the only thing I remember is hoping for a day off from school."

They all laughed at that.

For the next few hours the scene didn't change much, and neither did the hurricane's strength or course. It appeared they would get a direct hit if it didn't change course before long.

Nikki caught Mrs. Preston watching Russ and her, and she wondered what she thought about Russ' bringing her to share her home for the night or what she thought about seeing Russ with a woman at all. Even though Nikki had long been a friend to Russ and MaryAnn, Nikki wondered if Mrs. Preston thought they were now a couple.

How could she tell Mrs. Preston they were only friends?

But then again, how did she know?

Mrs. Preston stood up. "I think Libby and I will get our baths. Who knows if we'll have water later on tonight."

Libby grumbled as she slid out of the chair and followed her grandmother.

"I've put one of the kerosene lanterns and a flashlight in your bedroom, Mom. Call me if you need anything."

She leaned over and kissed Russ on the forehead, then looked him straight in the eye. "Be careful."

Chapter Eight

Hammerhead followed Mrs. Preston and Libby down the hall, leaving Russ and Nikki alone. Russ watched the TV, and Nikki looked at anything but Russ.

Suddenly he stood up. "Let's go sit in the den. I think we might as well get comfortable, unless you'd like to try to get some sleep."

"No, there's no way these eyes are going to close now. If you'll excuse me, though, I think I'll make a stop at the washroom first."

When she came out, she made her way quietly down the hallway, where she stopped to look over the wall of family photographs. A young Mr. Preston posed with a string of fish in one of the pictures. Nikki remembered Russ' dad. Russ looked a lot like him, tall and handsome with wavy brown hair. A small boy with huge brown eyes and blond curls sat on the ground with his own little string of fish.

Nikki followed Russ' childhood from T-ball and high school football to cap-and-gown photos of high school and college graduations. Then she stopped, surprised that a wedding picture of Russ and MaryAnn still hung on the wall. They posed in front of a little white chapel. Tall and slender with raven black hair, MaryAnn held her attention. Next to her was a group picture, with herself as the maid of honor, David, the best man, standing on the other side of Russ.

The years fell away. Nikki remembered how close she'd felt to Russ and MaryAnn that day. She remembered looking across the altar at David. Glancing up, he'd caught her gaze and winked.

How happy they'd all been. Their whole lives awaited them with the hopes and dreams of all young couples.

Russ' words came back to her: *Things change.*

With a sigh Nikki pulled her gaze away from the pictures on the wall. Things *had* changed—more than she'd ever imagined they would.

Before walking away she quickly scanned another small grouping of family photos of Gayle's children and little Libby as a baby.

Bands tightened around her heart for Russ. How had he coped?

Nikki forced herself to turn away and find Russ.

The den, small and cozy, hadn't changed much from

the years when the two couples were in high school. The browns and subtle golds and beiges in the couch and two chairs welcomed her. How many nights had they sat here watching movies or playing board games?

Tonight the room still offered her the warmth and security it had in her high school years. A candle and a small box of matches lay on the table at one end of the couch. Russ sat on the floor and flipped from the weather station to local reports.

"There's a couple of light blankets over there by the TV. Pull them out. Whether it's cold or not, they just seem to belong on the couch when the TV's on."

She carried the blankets to the couch and sat down.

After a long moment of silence Russ left to tuck in Libby. Sitting alone, Nikki listened to the wind whipping through the trees around the house. She pulled a blanket around her, fidgeted with the edge of it, then couldn't stand to sit still any longer.

She walked over to a window to peek out the blinds, amazed at how quickly the wind had strengthened. As if pulled by a powerful magnet, the trees and shrubs at the back of the house leaned toward the north, straining and bending with the force of the gale. Sheets of rain, sometimes heavy, sometimes lighter, swept across the lawn in a sideways motion almost parallel with the ground.

The hair on her neck tingled as Russ stepped up behind her.

"When we were little, Gayle and I used to fight over

who would have charge of the one flashlight that Dad owned. I guess that was Dad's way of making us feel we had an important job during a storm." His voice was soft and low. "We'd sit by this window together until the first bolt of lightning would light up the sky, and then Gayle would hightail it to find Mom."

He cleared his throat. "Tell me what happened to you and David."

Nikki snapped her head around to face him. "Wow! That was an abrupt change of subject."

"It's going to be a long night. Might as well catch up on our pasts."

Did she really want to dredge up memories of her failed marriage?

"I don't know where to start." She stared back out the window for a few seconds, then turned slightly so she could see Russ.

She took a deep breath. "Things changed between us, Russ. After a few years together he made it big in sales, bought the car dealership, and spent practically his entire life away from home. We never talked anymore. I never knew what he was thinking or doing half the time."

"That's not too uncommon. Couples grow apart all the time."

"But good marriages bring them back together. Our gap just kept growing." Consciously she pushed aside the deep hurt she felt creeping into her heart.

She shook the feeling and continued. "I think I realized

it after I spent a few weeks in California helping my parents move to their retirement home. When I got back, I sensed that things had gone from bad to worse. I couldn't pinpoint it, but the feeling was there." She didn't mention her later visit to him and MaryAnn and Libby.

Russ didn't comment, but a muscle in his jaw twitched.

Again she turned toward the window. "One of my friends pulled me aside and gave me the heads-up that David was running around on me. I was devastated but not completely surprised. Down deep in my heart I had suspected it for some time. I guess I didn't want to face it. I loved David and wanted our marriage to work."

She got quiet as she watched the trees sway.

"I guess it's good you didn't have children," Russ said quietly.

"David was never ready to have children." She tried to sound as if it was no big deal, but she was sure her eyes told another story.

"What about Nikki? Was she ready?" He put a hand on her arm as he asked. The automatic gesture seemed to come from his heart, and even though he might not have been aware of what he was doing, the kindness touched her deep inside.

She tried to smile. "Nikki had been ready for some time," she admitted, "but David had a difficult time accepting the idea that kids wouldn't interfere with his life. He said he had too much going on to raise children." Her eyes scanned the floor as her thoughts took her back in time.

Nikki finally looked up at Russ. "He said kids would've been in the way. With the business he said he needed me 'unencumbered' to help him." She laughed a little, ignoring the stab that always cut into her heart when she thought about her desire for a family of her own.

She inhaled deeply. "He liked to bring home guests—prospective big-bucks customers. He favored large dinner parties—with me doing all the work, of course. He bragged about my cooking, and I realized he was showing off all the things he had accumulated, with me at the top of the list."

Nikki watched Russ take in what she was saying about the man who'd once been like a brother to him. His eyebrows came together, and his lips tightened. Was he angry at his former friend for letting success go to his head, or was he upset with her for being part of David's change?

Not asking, or maybe not wanting to know, she continued. "I guess that's when I decided if we ever had a baby, it would become one of his possessions also. Of course, he was dead set against having children at the time. He said one day we'd talk about it."

She turned toward the window. Her voice was low. "Talking to David about anything was impossible if it wasn't his idea. I guess not being able to discuss things was the beginning of our breakup."

The sky lit up, and thunder roared. She wrapped her arms around herself and shivered.

"Enough about David. Let's go sit down." Russ led her to the big chair next to the couch. "I should've picked up some cards so we'd have something to help pass the time." He eased down onto the couch and stretched his long legs out in front of him, putting his hands behind his head.

"You're lucky to have Libby, and she's a lucky little girl to have you. You two make a great team."

"I thank my lucky stars every day that I have her. She makes me feel complete." As usual, his face lit up when he mentioned his daughter. "Raising her alone isn't exactly an ideal situation, but I guess we don't always get what we want, do we?"

"That's for sure," she said quietly.

Lost in their own thoughts, they sat and listened to the wind until something, probably a large branch, crashed against the roof. Nikki jumped.

"If you're uncomfortable there, you can come over here." He smiled. "I won't bite."

She hesitated, and then another "something" hit the house. Grabbing her blanket, she crawled up next to him, pulled her knees up to her chest, and drew the blanket around her. He didn't move. Neither did she.

Finally she broke the silence. "This reminds me of the day on Horn Island when we got caught in that afternoon storm."

Russ straightened up and seemed to relax. "Yeah, I

remember. We were catching so many trout that David and I didn't want to leave. You and MaryAnn were furious when the winds started."

"Oh, yeah. And we had good reason to be upset. We knew the weather was getting bad. You two wouldn't listen."

He grinned. "But wasn't it cozy when we had to huddle under the beach towels for almost an hour?"

Remembering, she chuckled. "Until the lightning popped. Scared us to death."

His eyes twinkled. "That's when it was the coziest. You and MaryAnn couldn't have gotten any closer to us."

Russ relaxed against the back of the couch once again and pulled her close to him.

He looked so content with the world, but Nikki . . . Nikki could hear her heart thumping. She had been nervous alone in the big chair because of the weather, but now there was no way to relax being this close to Russ.

Her insides churned. This wasn't the way it was supposed to be. Russ was like a brother to her.

She had to move.

Pulling away, she looked toward the hall. "Do you think your mom and Libby are okay?"

"Yes, but we can go check on them if it makes you feel better."

"It would."

They headed down the same hallway where she had just been. When they passed the pictures, Russ pointed out a few with his sister and him, but he made no mention of the wedding portrait or the picture of the happy couple holding a newborn.

He opened his mom's door, and they both peeked in. "Look. They're tucked in like two peas in a pod. Hammerhead's even in bed with them at their feet. They'll be fine. Believe me, Mom'll call if she needs us."

They started back down the hall, but before they got to the den, the lights went out. Total darkness enveloped them.

"Heck," he grunted, and he reached for Nikki.

"It's so dark" was all she said.

He found her arm and pulled her close to his body. "I can't believe I didn't carry a flashlight." Grumbling, he tucked her under his arm.

"Our eyes will adjust to the darkness in a minute," she said hopefully.

"You think so, huh?"

They shuffled along, every movement making her more aware of his arm across her shoulders. At one point she tripped and would've hit the floor had Russ not caught her and pulled her to him. She automatically put her arm around his waist. It was a mistake to lean toward him, but she knew of nothing else to do. Since he didn't seem to notice, she didn't try to pull away.

"I think we're almost there. I might be dreaming, but I think that's the couch over there and—ouch."

"And this is the chair, right?"

"Right. Mom keeps moving the furniture around."

He held her close, too close. Finally they reached the front of the couch.

She breathed a sigh of relief. "Guess we should've known the electricity would go off."

"Yeah, there'll be a lot of downed lines. Here, sit down."

She needed to get away from his touch. Confusion twisted her insides as she eased onto a sofa cushion. "Don't trip," she said as she felt him move away.

"I know those candles were here a minute ago."

She heard him fumble in the darkness, then saw the flash of a match and the flickering of a wick. His features glowed in its light, and she wanted nothing more than to take his face into her hands and . . .

She looked away. What was she thinking? This storm was playing havoc with her good sense. Remembering her friend's beautiful wedding portrait in the hall, she closed her eyes and willed the bolt of guilt to disappear.

Nonsense. That marriage no longer exists, and MaryAnn can't be considered a good friend any longer.

But even knowing her thoughts were true, her conscience still stung.

Russ placed the candle on the coffee table, picked up a blanket, and covered her. For a long moment their gazes remained riveted to each other. Neither said a word; then he sat next to her and pulled her into his embrace.

At first she stiffened and wanted to run. She couldn't. Instead, she leaned into Russ and snuggled against him.

Nikki looked up just as he lowered his mouth to hers. A sigh slipped from her throat as she closed her eyes and gave in to the sensation of total happiness that swept through her. For the moment it didn't matter what their pasts had been. The warmth of his lips against hers and the hand that ran along the length of her arm were all that mattered.

Never in her wildest dreams could she have imagined that Russ Preston would ever kiss her—not like this. Not like he loved her.

That thought sent a wave of confusion from her head to her toes.

Her head slid into his neck, and she began to tremble. "Russ, this wasn't supposed to happen," she said barely audibly. Tears welled in her eyes from sheer frustration.

What had she just done? What message had she sent to him? To herself?

Russ held her close, his breathing sporadic, his heart thumping.

"It's okay, Nikki," he whispered as if reading her thoughts. "I shouldn't have kissed you, but I couldn't stop myself. Even with my little girl and mother in the next room, I just couldn't stop myself. I had to kiss you. Hold you."

"Then just hold me."

She slid into his arms again, and he held her as if their short interlude would be over forever when the storm ceased. She felt it in his grip. She heard it in his breathing. In his way, he was saying good-bye before he had given them a chance.

Groaning, she laid her head on his chest and memorized the feeling of being near him.

She lay in his arms, pretending their time together would never end. The winds of the hurricane whirled around the house, lightning struck, and thunder crashed, but she heard nothing but the thumping of his heart.

Chapter Nine

A tree limb scraped against the roof of the house, jerking both Nikki and Russ out of their moment. Whether they had dozed or simply drifted into that semi-conscious space of time that only lovers know, it had to end.

"Nikki, we need to get up. Surely Mom heard that too."

"I know. We should've gotten up long ago. But—"

Russ stopped her as he lowered his head, kissing her soft and slow. She struggled to breathe as joy and sorrow clashed within her chest.

"Stay here," he said. "I'm going to get us something to drink."

As soon as he walked away from her, she felt more alone and confused than she had ever felt in her life. Two years ago, after her divorce, she'd sworn not to jump into another relationship. Living and doing for David was all she had known. Now it was time to know herself.

She nearly laughed out loud.

Relationship? What was she thinking?

Good gracious. The storm must have blown away my good sense.

Russ had kissed her. That's all. Men and women kissed all the time with no strings attached. Some of her friends talked about their dates, and Nikki knew they didn't expect a relationship.

Nikki plopped against the back of the couch and sighed. She knew she'd read too much into what had happened. She hadn't been kissed in so long. Even in the last couple of years with David, there had been precious little affection. Russ had simply reminded her of what she'd been missing.

Vowing to get control of herself, she straightened up and smoothed her hair as she listened to Russ in his mother's kitchen.

Russ stared at the glass in the sink now overflowing with water. He turned off the faucet. A sick feeling pulled at the pit of his stomach.

He had kissed Nikki—and not like a friend or a sister.

He snatched the two glasses out of the sink, then mopped them off.

Way to go. You finally allow someone to get close to you, and you act like a kid in junior high.

Taking a moment to calm his breathing, he resolved to do better. Nikki might be someone he could get involved with, but right now he couldn't afford to strain their friendship or, more important, to ignore his daughter in order to start a social life. The child was finally coming around. He couldn't risk ruining what he'd worked so hard to fix.

He swung open the door to the den but hesitated. Nikki sat on the couch, bent over with her head in her hands.

"Heck." Her muffled voice was barely audible. "Why can't life be simple?"

Russ swallowed hard. He'd upset her. He blew out a big swish of air before making his presence known.

"Talking to yourself?" He juggled both glasses, hoping he didn't look as uncertain as he felt. "Talking to yourself isn't necessarily bad, but sometimes it helps to talk to someone else."

He sat down next to her. After handing her a drink and placing his own glass on the coffee table, he took her chin in his hand. "We really do need to talk."

She sat perfectly still. She looked so vulnerable, he wanted to kick himself.

He picked up his glass, fidgeted with it for a second, then stood up. "I'm not sure what just happened between us, but I have to tell you, it started the first day I saw you standing on the pier. I've been fighting it ever since. I don't want to cause you any problems. Heck, I don't want to cause me problems either, so I think we need to understand each other." He turned and faced her.

Nikki took a sip from her glass, then looked him in the eye. "Yes, we do. I didn't come down here for this to happen. I want you to believe that. I came down here to restart my own life. I don't want to rely on anyone right now."

She watched him swallow hard before he answered.

"I understand."

"You really do, don't you?"

"Yes, I think I do. After my divorce everybody seemed to have just the right answer for all my problems. They tried to tell me how to live my life, how to find another wife, what to do about Libby. But I realized something. It was up to me to find the answer, or path, or whatever you want to call it."

He surprised her by again reaching out and lifting her chin with one finger. "I understand that you're looking for your answer, and I don't want to interfere."

"Thank you, Russ. You've always understood me. And you're right about people wanting to find the answers for you. After the news about David and me hit the West Coast, Mother told everyone. I had aunts calling me from across the country with just the right young man for me. It got to be almost funny."

"For you too, huh? I thought I was the only one caught in the curse of the matchmakers." He smiled. "But I'm not trying to fix you up with anyone. I'd be crazy to do that."

"Yeah?"

"Yeah. And I'm not asking you to rely on me to find

that path of yours, but it would be nice if you let me help."

"How? By kissing me?"

"Ooooh, that hurt." He grimaced.

"I didn't mean to hurt you. I guess I could use your help, but we've been friends a long time, Russ. I don't want to do anything to mess that up."

"And I don't want to do anything to ruin that either." He ran his hand across his chin. "So you think kissing might mess up our friendship up, do you?"

"I don't know what to think."

"I think you do. I think you feel the same way I'm feeling, but you're afraid to let it happen."

Sitting so close to Russ made her want to lean into him once more, to feel the warmth of his lips and the strength of his body.

But she knew what that would lead to. "It's too soon, Russ. Way too soon."

"Too soon since what?"

"Since I got here. Too soon since I've started trying to get back on my feet, and way too soon for your daughter, it seems."

Russ opened his mouth to say something, then stopped. His gaze moved from her across the dark room, then back to her. "I think you might have something there. Libby's had a hard time of it. She's really close to me now. Probably too close, but her doctors tell me it's natural for her to attach herself to me that way. They feel sure it'll get better as she starts to get involved in school activities again. For so long she couldn't do too much."

"I know. She's had a horrible time. That's why I don't want to be the one to cause her any more problems."

"She's a tough little girl. She's going to come around."

"Right now she sees me as the enemy. Maybe she thinks I'm trying to take her mother's place or squeeze her out of her relationship with you. Whatever she's feeling toward me isn't what I'd hoped for. She needs time."

He nodded. "I think I said that time was a healer. I guess we'll see if it heals her as well."

What could she say? Nikki felt as though she'd closed the door on any hopes of going beyond a friendship with Russ. Maybe it was for the best. His friendship meant the world to her, and she didn't want to damage it in any way.

They both straightened up as if they'd come to the same conclusion.

He cleared his throat. "I've got to check on Mom. Come with me. I promise I'll be good." He tried to change the mood by giving her one of his big smiles.

"Is my hair wild?" she asked as she felt it with her hands.

"Yep," he teased.

"Wait. Help me." She worked her fingers through her hair. "Where is it sticking out?"

"All over." He reached out and slowly smoothed her spiraling curls with his large hands. She closed her eyes and turned her head and kissed his hand.

Russ groaned as he pulled her into his arms. "I don't think a little kiss will ruin this friendship," he said as he brought his mouth down on hers.

But the kiss wasn't little. It was intense but much too short. Quickly he pulled away from her, then brushed her hair back with tenderness.

"Come on, let's go check on Mom and Libby. I think I'll wake them up if they're asleep. We could use a little company in here." He tried to make light of the subject, but Nikki heard a different note.

In her heart she knew he was as confused as she was. Neither of them had had much experience with a relationship lately or even in the past. MaryAnn had been his only love, and David had been hers.

He started to get up, but she touched his arm. "Maybe it's best that we do take it easy and just let things happen. Things usually work out for the best anyway, don't they?"

"You're right. Things do usually do work out." Even in the dim light of the candle, his eyes sparkled.

He took her into the kitchen first. Striking a match, he carefully lifted the glass globe from a kerosene lantern. With just a touch of the match, the wick ignited and lit the entire room. "Now we won't be in the dark."

He was wrong. Nikki felt more in the dark now than she had been before the night started.

She wished that solving her dilemma would be as easy as lighting a lantern.

They left the yellow flame of the lantern flickering in the kitchen and used a flashlight to walk down the hallway to Mrs. Preston's room.

"I was beginning to wonder if you had forgotten about us in here," Mrs. Preston said from the bed after Russ stuck his head in the doorway.

"No, Mom, we didn't forget about my two favorite ladies. We both dozed off for a few minutes. It's getting worse outside, so I think we ought to be together."

Nikki watched the scene unfold in front of her—the man, rough and rugged from tackling the elements every day, gently helping his gray-haired mother out of the bed with a tenderness she had not witnessed in a male before, then lifting his sleeping daughter to his chest and kissing her. Libby didn't stir.

Tough, physical work had hardened Russ's six-foot frame, but it hadn't hardened his nature. His rough hands could lift his mother gently or smooth a flyaway curl on her own head as softly as a sea breeze at dusk. The sea and wind and sky had honed his love of the natural and the beautiful, and that love was present even here in this dimly lit bedroom.

"Well, Nikki, did this storm bring back memories?" Mrs. Preston asked as she stood up.

"Oh, yes, ma'am. Lots of memories—and lots of noise. It's loud, very loud."

Mrs. Preston and Russ both laughed.

"Yes, hurricanes do tend to get rather noisy," Mrs. Preston agreed.

"Come on, Mom. Let's go into the den. I want to listen to the radio to see where our friend Bertram is." Hammerhead stretched his massive frame. "Come on, Hammerhead."

They settled in the den with the light of the lantern softening the objects around them. Russ placed Libby on the couch and tucked a blanket around her. Sitting on the floor next to her, he tuned in the battery-operated radio until he found the local civil defense director speaking. Bertram was right off the coast to the east of Biloxi and would make landfall within the hour.

"Well, we're in the worst of it. I hope my boat rides this out okay."

"How far away is it?" Nikki was making herself comfortable on the other end of the couch.

"We took several charter boats up not too far from here in the bayou. There's a narrow inlet where we tie the boats to the trees on both sides of the bayou and use about five anchors buried in the mud to keep them from going anywhere. Sometimes we lash several boats together. Yesterday I tied up with only one other boat. It usually works as long as lightning or wind doesn't take your trees away."

With the radio's hurricane advisories as a backdrop to what Russ was describing, Nikki could envision him struggling with ropes as he raced against time to get his boat secure. "Sounds risky—and muddy."

"It is, but it's better than leaving the boats in the harbor. It does get a little nasty trying to get the anchors in and out of the bayou mud—I don't particularly care for that part of it—but it's the best we can do."

Pulling her knees up to her chest, she placed her sock-clad feet on the couch and thought about the life Russ had carved out for himself and his daughter.

The wind roared as it swept through the trees and around the other structures on the street. It drove the rain into the sides of the house.

Nikki cringed. "Has the wind ever blown the windows out here?"

Mrs. Preston answered by telling her stories of different hurricanes and how the family rode them out. "Now in 1969 and in 2005 we went to Hattiesburg and stayed in a college dorm. Those storms were bad even up there. Took years to rebuild from those."

"Don't scare her, Mom. Storms like that don't happen often, and this isn't one of them."

"It's nice to know that this isn't a bad one, but I've got to tell you, it sounds bad to me."

"But back to your question, no, this house has never had anything but minor damage, not even a window blown out."

Nikki tried to smile, but she was afraid her uncertainty about everything, including the storm, showed. The look in Russ' eyes said he understood.

He got up and walked to a window as Nikki followed him with her gaze. Had Mrs. Preston not been in the room with her, she would have physically followed him, but instead she leaned her head against the back of the couch and closed her eyes.

A little later she found herself curled up on the couch with a pillow under her head and a warm blanket over her. Something was different. No sound, no wind, no rain.

She sat up. "Is it over?"

"Unfortunately, no. This is the eye," Russ explained as he stepped through the door of the hallway. "Once this small quiet zone passes us, we'll have the other side of the storm, but it shouldn't be as bad."

"What time is it?"

"It's three-thirty. It should be over by daybreak, because the backside of this one isn't as widespread as the front side. Would you like to lie down in a bed?"

"No, unless I'm in the way here."

He smiled. "Not at all. I just tucked Mom and Libby back in."

"Russ, have you had any rest? You'll be dead tired tomorrow if you don't get some sleep."

"I think I'll try to close my eyes for a few minutes while it's calm." He hesitated. "Mind if I sit by you?"

She nodded. "You look exhausted. Please, sit."

Russ sat near her but not close enough for their bodies to touch. With his head relaxed against the back of the couch, he turned, his eyes burning into hers. Neither said a word. He reached for her hand and held it on her lap. Within minutes he was asleep.

Nikki rested her head against the sofa back and watched Russ sleep. He was a man comfortable with his place in the world. He had survived an ordeal with his daughter that could have soured his outlook on life. Instead, he seemed to be at peace.

She rubbed a finger across the callused skin of his thumb. Hard work had toughened his body, but the tough life that he'd lived had formed the character of the man she admired. With her hand in his, she felt comforted and safe. Sleep came to her as well.

By morning the winds had subsided as the storm moved away from the coastline. When Nikki opened her eyes, she saw Russ sitting at the kitchen table talking on his cell phone. When he hung up, he started toward her.

Running her fingers through her hair, Nikki sat up and tried to make herself presentable, a formidable task without electricity and a blow dryer.

"Just got off the phone with Gayle and Mickey," Russ said as he sat down next to her. "They made out just fine."

Mrs. Preston stepped into the den. "Morning, Nikki." She lifted a hand in greeting as she headed for the hallway.

Russ waited until his mother left, then pulled Nikki against him. "Morning. I'm glad you got some sleep."

"Me too. It was a long night."

For a moment Nikki allowed herself the comfort of having his arm around her. How wonderful to wake up to such a pleasure, she thought. But then she remembered where she was and sat up straight.

He kissed her on the nose and stood up.

"It was a long night but interesting." She stretched and stood up beside him. "I'd forgotten how dark the night gets and how grating a storm can be on the nerves."

"I agree with that. There's nothing pleasant about a hurricane. I was on my way to get the butane burner to make some coffee. That ought to cheer you."

"Sounds good. What can I do to help?"

He looked at her more closely. "Nothing. I'll be out on the back porch, but if you want, you can freshen up first."

"I look that bad, huh?" Nikki glanced down at her rumpled clothes.

"I'm not crazy enough to answer that."

Playfully she nudged him. "Smart man."

After taking a detour to the restroom and managing to pull her hair back in a rubber band, Nikki walked out onto the porch. A pot of water bubbled on a butane stove, and cups, instant coffee, and a package of cinnamon rolls were laid out beside it. Russ came from around the house.

"Any damage?" she asked.

"Just a lot of downed branches. Nothing bad." He came up onto the porch beside her. He had changed into jeans and a red T-shirt, and even with a shadow on his face from a needed shave, he looked handsome. "Let's have some coffee."

She scooped a teaspoon of instant coffee into a cup

and added the hot water. She took a drink. "I wonder if the condos are okay."

"We'll see in a few minutes, but I'm sure everything is just fine. As soon as we finish this makeshift breakfast, we'll try to get there."

"I guess the roads will be covered with fallen limbs and junk."

"More than likely, but we'll try it anyway." There was an awkward silence as they sat and sipped their morning coffee. Nikki wanted to say something about their conversation last night, but nothing seemed appropriate in the light of day.

By his silence she guessed that Russ felt the same way. Total relief spread through her when Libby stepped out the screen door.

"Good morning, princess. Did you hear the wind last night?"

Libby shook her head. She reached for a roll, but Russ pulled her into his arms. "No breakfast without a kiss for your dad first."

"Daaaad," she whined, but she didn't pull away.

Russ kissed her on top of her head, then let her go. "I'll get you some milk from the ice chest."

Russ left Nikki alone with Libby. Libby grabbed a cinnamon roll and plopped down in a plastic chair.

The sweet smile that she had given Russ just seconds before turned into a pout. Nikki wasn't sure what the right approach would be, but she certainly wasn't going to miss the opportunity to talk to the girl.

"Your grandmother certainly bragged about you, Libby. She was telling me about how you help her around the house. I think that's wonderful. So many young girls don't want to take the time to learn from their grandparents."

Libby took a big bite of roll and nodded without actually looking at Nikki.

Refusing to give up, Nikki picked up a roll and pulled another chair near the girl. "Your dad has nothing but praise for you as well. He was telling me that you're going to play softball this year with the city league. I did that when I was about your age. I wasn't very good at it, but I remembered I made a lot of good friends and had fun."

"Yeah. I can't wait."

Nikki had hoped for more, but at least the girl answered her.

Russ opened the door. "Here's some milk. Nikki, do you need anything else?"

"No, I'm ready to help get things in order for your mom."

Nikki really wanted to sit and have a conversation with Libby, but she had a feeling that even if she stayed longer with the girl, the conversation would be one-sided at best.

Within thirty minutes Russ and she had picked up fallen branches close to the walkways around the house and had put out some chairs and other necessities for Mrs. Preston. The rest could wait until Russ or Mickey came over later.

With Libby buckled into the truck's small backseat, Nikki and Russ waved good-bye to Mrs. Preston. Hammerhead sat between them on the front seat.

They met only a few other cars out on the road. Russ took his time, carefully dodging fallen limbs, wires, and signs that littered the streets. Several policemen stopped them to question where they were going, but Russ was able get permission to continue. In fact, one of the officers knew Russ and asked about his family.

They made it to Nikki's condo in less time than it had taken them to get to Mrs. Preston's the day before. Everything seemed to be intact, and Nikki let out a sigh of relief as they all stepped out of the truck. Hammerhead and Libby ran ahead of them.

"Well, I guess life goes back to normal tomorrow, huh?" she commented. "It doesn't appear that there was any real damage along here, just a lot of junk blown around." Piles of seaweed that had washed up onto the road and into parking complexes littered the beachfront area. Nikki was glad that her car had been on the garage's second floor.

Russ took a minute, then commented, "Depends what you mean by normal."

Surprised, Nikki looked up at him and understood. It's exactly what she had been thinking earlier but was afraid to say. Her life wouldn't be the same again either. "When will I see you again?"

"I'm not sure. I have a full schedule this week if my

charters don't cancel, but call me if you need me for your hotel guests. I might be able to fit another charter in."

Nikki wasn't asking about work and charters and fishing, but she'd never tell him that right now. Obviously their night together didn't mean as much to him as it did to her.

She nodded. "I'll call—or, better yet—call me if you have an opening."

Russ looked as if he realized she was putting the ball into his court. It would be up to him to call her.

He nodded, then picked up her television and carried it inside.

Nikki looked around and breathed a sigh of relief. "Home, sweet home. Thanks goodness everything is okay."

"I'm glad for you." He checked all the windows for her, then headed toward the door. "I'll see you around, Nikki. I'm going to Gayle's, then I need to check on my other girl."

It took her a moment to realize he was talking about *The Half-Moon*.

With a big smile he winked. "Got to make sure she rode it out okay, or I won't have a job tomorrow."

Chapter Ten

Life did get back to normal for the people on the Gulf Coast. Within a week most signs of Bertram had vanished, even though the tourist business took a nose-dive. The storm, as always, had scared away some potential travelers.

Nikki preferred having a hectic schedule, one that kept her too busy to think about Russ, but she took what her days offered and tried to make the most of them. With fewer charters, she avoided having to call him, but in her heart she longed to pick up the phone.

Several times a day and especially at night when she was alone, Nikki did exactly that. She'd reach for the phone, rub her thumb across the top—the way he'd rub his thumb across her chin—then take a step back. What would she say if she called? Would he even answer?

He had made it clear that he didn't want to upset his daughter's progress. She had agreed and had even thrown in the fact that it was much too early for her to think about getting involved with someone.

What was she thinking?

So while everything else along the coast was as it was before the hurricane, Nikki knew things would never be the same for her.

On Tuesday of the following week Russ surprised her with a call. Seeing his name on the caller ID sent her heart soaring. She let it ring three times before picking it up, scared of what he might have to say.

Finally on the fourth ring she grabbed it before he gave up. Hearing whatever he had to say would be better than not knowing.

His voice warmed her. How had she ever thought he'd break off a beautiful friendship, even if it had nearly imploded with a kiss?

"You want me to spend a day with you and Libby on the boat?"

"Yeah. I thought you might have a good time. I have a day's charter scheduled. The guy's friends backed out, so I offered him half price if he'd share the boat with someone else. I use charters like this to take my friends and family out," Russ explained. "I've been promising Libby a fishing trip, and I thought this would be a good way for the two of you to get to know each other again."

"What does Libby say about having me on the boat with her?"

"She gave her usual reply—a shrug. She didn't jump for joy, but she didn't pitch a fit either. I've learned that, for a nine-year-old, that's a good sign."

"If you say so. I don't want to do anything that'll make things worse for her."

Silence.

"Russ, are you still there?"

"Yes, I'm still here. Uh, I had a little talk with my daughter. I'm not sure if that was the thing to do or not, but it's done now. I tried to explain that I needed to spend time with other people, adults, and some of them would be women."

"And? How did she handle that?"

"How else? A shrug. I'm trying to be a good dad, Nikki. I really am. But sometimes I feel like I don't have a clue what to do with a child."

"Captain Preston, you could win the Father of the Year Award for all you've done for Libby. Stop being so hard on yourself. Things will work out."

She heard him take a big breath. "So, will you join us on the boat?" he asked.

"Yes, I'd love to."

She hung up the phone with a smile.

That smile kept popping up throughout the rest of the day and into the night, but by 5:30 the next morning, as she drove through the deserted streets toward the harbor, the smile was replaced with a prayer on her lips and a sinking feeling in her heart.

Would Libby resent her being on the boat? She

hoped not. She prayed that the three of them could find common ground so she could keep seeing Russ. She knew that she and Russ could continue their friendship, but after the kiss on the night of the storm, Nikki was afraid she wanted more than friendship from him.

Today, though, she'd enjoy the trip, and she hoped Libby would do the same.

She pulled into the parking lot. The harbor's morning quiet differed from the chaos she'd come to expect in the afternoons. Only one other crew loaded supplies onto a boat. *The Half-Moon* glistened in the hazy glow of a streetlight. Her chrome and stainless steel shone through the early-morning fog that hovered lightly just above the watercraft.

A feeling of peace and serenity settled over Nikki as she parked next to Russ' truck.

Russ stepped halfway out of the cabin wearing his usual khaki shorts, T-shirt, and boat shoes. He turned and spoke to someone inside. Nikki guessed it was Libby, since Joey was working with fishing equipment on the back deck. Hammerhead lay at his feet.

When he closed the door behind him, Russ spotted her getting out of her car. His big grin told her that everything would be okay today. Waving, she grabbed her bag.

"Good morning." Russ grabbed a rope and pulled the boat closer to the pier. "You look spry. Ready for some fishing?"

"I am. I can't wait." She handed him her bag, then

waited for him to help her onto the boat. After tossing the bag onto the deck, he held her hand and put his other near her waist as she stepped on board. It took more control than she thought she'd have not to slide into his embrace and let him hold her.

Instead, she stepped back. For a moment his eyes narrowed. He stood, unmoving, looking as if he'd been stopped in the middle of an action. Had he wanted to pull her into an embrace? Maybe give her a good-morning kiss?

Her heart fluttered at the thought, but before she found something to say to break the ice, he reached down and grabbed her bag. "Come on inside and say good morning to Libby."

Libby sat in the captain's chair inside the cabin. She spun around and waved as Nikki stepped into the cabin with Russ.

That's a good start, thought Nikki. *A wave is better than a frown.* Crossing her fingers, she prayed that this would be the day she'd get close to Russ' daughter.

Russ must have been down at the pier for hours, because within minutes of her arrival the boat was heading out of the harbor. Libby, Hammerhead, and Mr. Lawson, the one guest, took their places on the back deck.

Nikki settled against the cushioned back of one of the fighting chairs, turning it so she could see the cabin and the bridge above her. The cool morning air gently swirled around her. Russ stood at the wheel on the bridge. Even though she tried, she couldn't take her eyes off the muscular arms that skillfully maneuvered the boat out into the channel. Russ waved to several other boaters and talked to one on the VHF.

She tried not to be conspicuous, but he must have sensed her watching him. He turned.

"If you get tired," he shouted down to her, "you can lie down up front. We'll wake you when we get to the rigs."

"No thanks. I'm fine right now. I wouldn't miss this scene for the world. It's so peaceful. It's been a long time since I've been on the water at daybreak."

He nodded, then concentrated on the water ahead of him.

As the boat left the lights of the harbor and the beachfront, the few remaining stars shone above her. Nikki leaned her head against the chair back and lost herself in the silence and vastness of the heavens. Closing her eyes, she let the vibrations of the diesels lull her until a floating sensation weaved its way from her head to her toes.

"Enjoy your nap?" Russ sat next to her in a companion fighting chair.

"What?" Wiping her eyes, she stifled a yawn.

Libby was standing on the back deck, watching the sky to the east, where the sun was beginning to rise.

"I think you dozed off, but I woke you so you wouldn't snore in front of my daughter."

"Russ, you know I wasn't snoring," she said in a whisper for only him to hear. But then she added, "Was I?"

"Oh, no, you'd never snore." He laughed and turned around.

Hints of pink stained the eastern sky, and Nikki repositioned her chair to watch. "I love a sunrise from a boat. I think they're even more beautiful than sunsets."

"I agree." Russ' gaze moved from her to the sky, where the colors of the morning gathered over the water. With the gentle vibration of the engines, the soft breeze caressing her skin, and the sky lighting up in front of her, Nikki felt at peace with the world, a feeling that had become foreign to her in recent years.

Russ looked up to the flying bridge and gave the signal for Joey to turn south and open throttle. The spell was broken.

"To think this happens every morning, and most of the world misses it."

"You're so right. Have you been on the bow yet?"

"No, but is it safe while we're going this fast?" She looked at the water streaming past her and cringed.

"Sure, if you hold on. Come on, you'll love it. Libby, want to join us?" Shaking her head, Libby sat down and began texting on her cell phone.

Nikki heard a sigh from Russ, but neither said a word. Instead, he took her arm, showed her where to hold on, and guided her to the front of the boat, where they leaned up against the cabin. The air was cooler here, with the wind hitting them directly in the face, and Russ placed an arm around her shoulders. Involuntarily she snuggled up against him.

"I remember how you used to talk about you and your friends fishing out here when you were young."

"Oh, yeah. I had two cousins about my age, and we literally lived out here. But it wasn't like this. We had an old skiff that we'd pull up under a pier on the beach. It didn't even have a motor. We each had a paddle, and we worked hard at getting where we wanted to go."

He quit talking, and Nikki knew he was lost to his memories. Even with her back to him, Nikki could imagine the smile that surely formed on his face. "Sounds like fun."

He chuckled. "Oh, yeah," he repeated. "Lots of evenings when we'd be paddling in, we'd see Mom standing on the beach, waving her arms ninety miles to nothing above her head. We knew she was yelling at us, but of course we couldn't hear what she was saying. She'd grab us by the ears when we got out of the boat and fuss all the way home about our being gone too long or being out in the rain and how I was turning her hair gray." He got very quiet.

"It sounds wonderful. I wish I'd known you then. I was probably dodging traffic with my parents in one of the big cities we lived in while you were out here enjoying all this."

"It was wonderful, all right."

As they stood on the bow of the boat with nothing to ward off the elements, the wind whipped against Nikki's body. She folded her arms around herself.

When a spray of cold water sent a shiver through her,

Russ pulled her closer. "Are you cold? Maybe we'd better go back and get you warm inside the cabin."

"No, I'm fine." It was better to tell a lie than to risk moving away from him. She wasn't fine. But she liked being next to him, letting him hold her, even knowing that nothing probably would ever come of it. Just like the night of the storm, when he'd fallen asleep holding her hand, Nikki felt secure in the knowledge that he was next to her.

"Yeah, me too." His voice was a whisper, but she caught the words before they vanished with the wind.

"But," he threw in in a louder voice, "I need to give Joey a hand."

Disappointed but understanding that he had a job to do and a paying guest on board, she stepped away from him. "Do you allow guests to ride in the flying bridge with you?"

"Sure, but you'll have to promise to behave."

She laughed. "I'll try."

He took her by the arm and led her to the stern of the boat and up the ladder. At the top, she swung onto the floor of the bridge and pulled herself up.

Joey turned around and smiled. She could tell he had a wad of gum in his mouth. "Hi, Miss Nikki. Great morning, huh?"

"It's a gorgeous morning, Joey."

Russ got his footing on the bridge and stepped up next to Joey. "I'll take the wheel if you'll go down and get the equipment ready and keep an eye on my daughter."

With a quick nod Joey swung himself down the ladder and disappeared.

"You sure I won't be bothering you if I stay up here? I don't want to do anything against your regular charter rules."

"No, I welcome visitors up here. Gets kind of boring being alone. But I can't promise you that you won't 'bother' me."

When he turned his head to face her, her breath caught in her throat. His meaning was much too clear. She grabbed a stainless steel bar to keep her balance, but she knew the dizziness wasn't coming just from the waves or the height of the flying bridge.

As the boat flew across the water, a wave of excitement zipped through her. Exhilaration such as she hadn't experienced in years awakened all her senses. "This is marvelous. So different from the calm cruise the other night."

Russ smiled. "Hold on the way you're doing for a few minutes, and you'll get the feel of it just like you did before."

With one hand holding down her cap, she closed her eyes and let the wind blow into her face. "We're going so much faster, but I love the breeze. I feel like I'm a teenager again on the front of your old boat. Free. Not a care in the world."

"Yeah, those were the days, weren't they?" He adjusted the controls, then continued. "If we want to get to the rigs today, we have to run pretty fast." He patted the seat. "Come sit by me. You'll feel a little safer than standing."

Nikki slid onto the bench next to him. The windshield kept the wind from hitting her, and she was able to relax and think about Russ' words. They were so true. She did feel safe next to him.

She looked up at him just as he turned toward her. Giving her a big smile, he patted her leg. "Enjoy the ride."

Nothing else was said as the boat headed south. The scenery thrilled her, but sitting next to Russ made the morning that much nicer.

Nikki watched the tree line of an island appear on the horizon. "Is that Horn Island?"

"Yep. You're good. I figured you'd get the islands mixed up after so long."

"I was taking a lucky guess. It felt like we were heading in the same direction you'd take us when we were kids."

The stared at the island as the boat ran along the channel at its western edge.

"Do you still come out here?"

He frowned. "Come to think of it, it's been years since I've been out here. I pass it a lot in the boat, but with all of Libby's operations, we didn't get a lot of island time."

"That's sad."

"You're right. It is. I've been so concerned about getting her body well, maybe I've neglected letting her be a little girl. We'll have to change that real soon. We'll bring her out to the island one day."

"I'd like that."

He looked down at Libby. "I hope she'll get into the fishing part of this trip. Maybe if she gets off the phone long enough to hold a pole, she'll enjoy herself."

"I imagine when we pull in our first fish, she'll throw that phone into the cabin and join us."

"I hope you're right."

She looked at him and grinned. "We *are* going to catch fish, aren't we?"

"Hey, you're on the best charter boat in the harbor, and you're with the luckiest captain on the water."

"Lucky, huh?"

This time he yanked his cap low on his forehead and speared her with his eyes. "Talk like that is not allowed in this flying bridge. It makes the captain nervous."

Realizing what her words had insinuated, Nikki swallowed hard. How could she ever treat Russ only as a friend if everything they said and did reminded her of their passionate kiss the night of the storm? He certainly wasn't making this easy for her. Even the gentle touch of his thigh against hers reminded her how closely they sat.

"I'm glad you came today," Russ finally said. "I hope you'll have a good time."

"I wouldn't have missed it. It's been a long time since I've been deep-sea fishing. Hope I remember how."

She wanted to tell him she'd have a good time just being with him on the boat, but she kept that tidbit of information to herself. Somehow she felt he knew it any way.

"It's like riding a bike. It'll all come back to you."

"Hope so. I want to catch some fish."

"I'll try my best to make that happen. Anything else I should try to do?"

She laughed. "Yes, try to behave in front of your daughter."

"I'll try to do that too."

Nikki's spirits soared just from being near him.

"What's up?" she asked when she saw the quirky curl of his lips. "You look like the cat that swallowed the canary."

"Nothing. Absolutely nothing is wrong. You just make me feel good."

"You make me feel good too."

"I have to get out of here." He stood up in front of the wheel. "Why don't you steer, and I'll go down to get the rods ready. Think you can handle that?"

"No problem." She saluted him and slid behind the wheel.

He stepped around her, then stood behind the bench. "Keep it heading about one-ninety south."

Nikki concentrated on watching the compass as she turned the wheel. "Am I on course?"

Russ bent over her and placed a hand on her shoulder to be able to see the compass. "Perfect," he said.

Nikki caught his eye—and the double meaning—as he gently massaged her shoulder.

When he lifted his hand, Nikki felt abandoned. She wanted to reach out to him.

Russ looked out across the water. "We're getting pretty close to the rigs. Yell if you think you need me back up here. I won't be far."

Russ left her with the power of the boat in her hands. With one tiny movement of the wheel, the boat would swerve. Sometimes she felt it go off course, but mostly she had to turn around to see the squiggly trail of foam behind her to realize she'd veered. Quickly she'd make adjustments, then concentrate on not turning the wheel too hard.

When the trail behind the boat straightened out, she relaxed and turned to see Russ helping Libby rig a fishing pole. Russ' smile reassured her that things would be okay.

If only she could reassure herself that her life would find its straight and narrow course as easily as the boat had.

The rest of the day brought highs and lows of emotions for Nikki. The massive legs of the oil rigs and the clarity of the water around them amazed her. Bending over the railing, she could see the clean, sandy bottom. It looked just inches away from the boat, but in reality she knew it was far below.

She and Libby shouted with excitement when schools of fish or a solitary crab swam by. She thrilled at the squeal of the reel when a fish struck, but she squirmed at the sight of the blood from their landed trophies.

Several times during their stay at the rigs Russ passed by her and placed a hand on her shoulder or elbow or showed her how to manage a rod.

"Here, hold it closer to your body. Put your hand here."

He stepped near her, wrapped his arms around her body, and positioned the fishing rod correctly. "You've got to have control. If that big one comes along, you have to be able to react before he gets away."

With his body next to hers, his warm breath on the back of her neck, and the rocking of the boat forcing her against him, Nikki had a hard time concentrating. She dug deep within herself to find the strength to keep from turning into his chest and letting him hold her.

But they weren't alone on the boat. Joey stood at the bow with their guest, and Libby fished just a few feet away from them.

"Dad, come show me."

"Sure thing." He released Nikki's pole and stepped near Libby.

Nikki watched him show his daughter the same hold he'd shown her. With patience he demonstrated how to position the pole just as he'd shown her minutes ago.

She hoped Libby truly needed help and wasn't feeling left out because Russ had not helped her first.

A squeal pierced the quiet. "Daddy! I've got one!"

Libby clung to the pole as it threatened to pop out of her hands. "Help me!" she yelled, but before the words were out of her mouth, Russ had a hand on the pole.

"Great job, Libby. I think you have a monster fish there."

Russ backed behind her and reached for the pole with his other hand. "You reel. I'll just help hold the rod."

Libby's smiles were contagious. Nikki quickly reeled in her line and put away her pole to give Libby her full attention. Russ and Libby managed to pull in a medium-sized spadefish. It wasn't the biggest Nikki had ever seen, but it was the most beautiful. Its stripes of different shades of gray and silver sparkled in the sun.

"Daddy, it's huge!"

"Yes, it is. Are you going to keep it?"

Libby looked at the fish, then up at Russ, her big brown eyes questioning. "Should I?"

Russ shrugged. "Well, these fish really aren't good eating. Sometimes we toss them back over and tell them, "Go grow."

"You do?"

"Yep, and sometimes, I swear, those same fish let us catch them on our next trip."

For a moment Nikki thought Libby wouldn't give the fish its freedom, but then she ran a little hand down its shiny back, lifted it in front of her face, and looked it straight in the eye. "Okay, fish. You got to let me catch you again on my next trip. So, go grow!"

With that, she tossed it over the side. At first it swam on its side, then, after several tries, straightened up and darted out of sight.

Everyone breathed a sigh of relief. Libby clapped.

"That was a wonderful thing you did, Libby," Nikki said. "That fish is on its way to getting really big."

Libby looked at her and beamed.

Finally I said something right. Nikki's heart warmed at the girl's smile.

The sun and the fishing took its toll on Nikki and Libby. When they headed in, Libby curled up in one of the fighting chairs and fell asleep. Nikki covered her with a beach towel to protect her from the sun. Nikki found the solitude in the V-bunk just what she needed. The vibrations and rocking of the boat put her to sleep almost immediately.

A warm kiss and a loving caress on her shoulder made Nikki's eyes flutter open. She knew they were Russ' lips before she opened her eyes. She smelled the day's salt on his skin and felt the faint beginnings of his afternoon shadow above his lip.

"Wake up, sleepyhead. We're almost home," he said as he pulled her close.

"I thought you were a dream," she whispered. The afternoon sun caught the glimmer in his eye. A quiver rippled through her.

Water beat against the bow of the boat as it sped across the surface of the water, and the beat of her heart became one with its motion. She wanted to lose herself in its rhythm, but, knowing they were not alone on the boat, she made herself pull away from him. She sat up.

Russ did the same but didn't get up. Instead he turned and leaned close. He traced the outline of her lips with delicate touches, much too soft for his big hands. "Hmm, does that mean you dream of me?"

Taking a moment to understand his question, she smiled up at him. "I'll never tell. She stretched and looked nervously toward the door.

"Relax. Libby's busy with Joey and Hammerhead. Our passenger is out back, half asleep," he whispered as his lips toyed with hers once again.

This time it was no dream. She returned his kiss, ever so slowly, until he pulled away. Her breath caught in her throat.

Cupping her face with both hands, he kissed her forehead.

"I didn't plan this, but when I saw you lying down here, I couldn't resist."

"I'm not sorry. I've been thinking about this all day."

A smile curled his lips. "You have, have you?"

"Daddy, what are you doing?"

Nikki and Russ jumped. Libby stood at the door of the cabin, her mouth wide open. "Daddy, what are you doing in bed with her?"

In seconds Russ slid off the bunk and knelt down by his daughter, his arms encircling her. "Baby, Miss Nikki and I were talking. I was sitting close to her because I like her. She and I are really good friends."

Libby's frown told Nikki that she wasn't falling for Russ' explanation.

"You were kissing her."

Nikki heard a quick breath escape from Russ, but within seconds he was back in control.

"And that's okay if a man kisses a lady he likes."

Libby shrugged out of his arms. With a quick spin, she stomped up the stairs.

Russ didn't try to stop her. Instead, he leaned back on his heels and threw his head back. "Girls."

"I'm sorry, Russ. I should've gotten up as soon as you came down here."

"Nonsense. We weren't doing anything wrong." He stood and stomped up the stairs after Libby. His voice, quiet but stern, drifted down to her.

"Please, God. Don't let me cause a problem for him."

Chapter Eleven

The wee hours of morning found Russ still awake. He tossed and turned, trying to get Nikki off his mind. He turned onto his side and jammed his arm under the pillow, but it only reminded him of Nikki's body as she leaned into him in the bunk. He turned on his back, but he could still feel her presence.

She'd been on the coast for only a month or so, and already he had kissed her twice, once during the hurricane and once on the boat. He had promised himself he wouldn't do anything to harm their friendship, but when he was with her, he couldn't treat her as only a friend.

He got up and walked to the kitchen for a glass of orange juice. *Love.* He never wanted to fall in love again, but no way could he stop the feelings for Nikki that grew stronger each time he saw her.

154

Everyone had told him that love would happen again, but he never listened, never believed it to be possible. Having his family break up had been the hardest thing he had ever lived through. Some men would treasure their freedom, but not him. Deep inside he knew he was a family man. That's why he strove so hard to make a decent home and to be a father and a mother for Libby.

He'd sworn never to put himself in a position to be hurt that badly again, yet Nikki had pulled emotions up from deep within him. She had made him feel alive again.

She had made him love again.

Friendship had turned into love so quickly that it frightened him. Nikki had never used the word *love* with him, but he felt sure that he wasn't reading her wrong. He sensed she was feeling the same emotions he was, but he wondered if they would last. She'd been divorced for only two years, and this was the first time she'd reached out to someone since. For her, would the feelings pass as quickly as they had begun?

With his hips against the countertop, he sipped his orange juice and let the quiet of the kitchen surround him. It wasn't hard to picture Nikki here with him. He loved the chaos of family life—probably why he loved going to his sister's. With only him and Libby, their condo was usually quiet and orderly—not a bad thing, but it wasn't a home filled with life.

The clock on the stove showed 3:00. He groaned. The mind did crazy things at three in the morning. His had just taken Nikki from being only a friend to being his—could he even think it?

He shook his head. Yep, the mind did crazy things at this time of the morning.

Going beyond friendship with Nikki would take work. First, he knew that battles loomed ahead for him with Libby. But he decided he was ready to face them. She was a child, and she would have to understand. He'd given her the last five years completely. Now it was time to let someone else into their lives.

His daughter would come around. It wasn't entirely her fault that she was so possessive of him. Being so protective of her throughout the years of her surgeries had made her the way she was. That would pass as she got to know Nikki better.

To convince Nikki that friends could fall in love might be a little harder.

He put the glass into the sink and went back to his bedroom to get dressed for that day's charter. A sinking feeling hit him in his gut. Why had he allowed himself to be so vulnerable? For five years he had kept a sturdy wall around him where women were concerned, and he had been content. Now, after having Nikki back on the coast, he wondered if he could ever go to bed alone again and not think of her.

Didn't he know better than to give his heart away? He would be the one to get hurt, and he would have no one to blame but himself.

No, he hoped he hadn't made a tremendous mistake to

let his guard down and fall in love with Nikki. Now he would have to deal with loving her, hoping she was ready.

He shook his head. It wasn't the future he'd planned, but he was ready to give it his best.

The hot days of July had quickly turned into the sultry days of August, but rather than hating the heat, Nikki thrived in it. Her hair curled tighter each day with the unrelenting humidity, but she learned to tie it up in a ponytail or twist or simply to wear a cap. She could deal with a little humidity if it meant being near the beach and water.

And, if she were honest with herself, being near Russ. Of course, since the fishing trip they had only talked on the phone, and Russ had been pleasant but not his usual jovial self.

Several times Nikki had asked if Libby was still upset with them.

"She's a child. She'll get over it" was his customary response.

Not exactly what she wanted to hear.

Deciding that Russ was too involved with his daughter's welfare to add complications to his life, she convinced herself that being his friend was the best she could hope for.

As she sat at her window watching the water and thinking about finding herself a hobby to keep her mind occupied, the telephone rang. She listened as Russ invited her to his condo to cook for her.

So much for finding something to keep her mind off him. Every time she tried to resolve the issue, Russ managed to tear a gaping hole in her plans.

To keep her sanity, she thought about refusing his invitation, but before her good sense kicked in, she accepted it. How could she say no when she hadn't gotten her mind off him since the boat trip?

The next day stretched into an eternity. She wanted it to end, but at the same time she feared the consequences of spending an evening with Russ. It would only make her feelings for him stronger and harder to get over if things didn't work out for the two of them.

Since his truck was in the shop, Russ asked her to pick him up at the harbor and take him to the garage before going to his condo.

When she saw him closing up the boat, her head felt light, and an uncontrollable smile spread across her face. Just seeing him was an unexpected comfort, like coming home and finding it hadn't changed.

Catching her eye, he hurried off the pier and leaned into the window of her car. "Hi." He gave her a quick kiss. "You look great."

She wanted to say that he looked gorgeous, but she didn't. "Thanks. I stayed in the air-conditioned office all day, so my hair is still somewhat under control."

He walked around the car and slid in.

"Are we stopping for Libby on the way?"

"No, she's sleeping at Gayle's tonight. She and Mickey are taking the kids to a movie."

She swallowed hard. They'd be alone. Not good. Not good at all.

Half listening, half worrying about the evening ahead, she tried to follow his conversation. Relief spread through her when he got into his own car at the garage. At least she had a few minutes to calm her nerves. By the time she pulled into his parking garage, she had her head on straight and was ready for a wonderful evening with a friend.

Like her own, Russ' condo complex sat on the beach side of the highway. He helped her out of the car, then escorted her to the elevator. She stood next to him in silence as she listened to the elevator glide down. Would he try to kiss her in the elevator?

She swallowed a groan before it slipped out.

This was going to be a really long night if she couldn't control herself.

The door opened. Nikki glanced up to Russ as she stepped in, expecting him to be smiling down at her. He wasn't. Instead, he touched her elbow as he always did to escort her and led her into the car with no expression on his face.

As the door closed, Russ took a step away from her and pushed the button for the third floor. Only then did he look at her and smile.

So much for kisses, she thought. Relief should have washed over her. It didn't.

Neither said a word as the elevator whooshed its way to his floor. Had she done something to offend him?

Was he bringing her here tonight to tell her he couldn't see her anymore?

Her heart, which had beaten with excitement only moments before, now thudded against her chest. She wrapped her arms around herself and lowered her gaze until the beep for the third floor made her look up.

His eyes had darkened. He hesitated, then took a step out of the car, breaking the tension. "Here it is. Not high enough to be the penthouse, but it gives me a nice view of the channel."

They were the first words he'd spoken since they stepped into the parking lot. She blinked, then looked around him to see the coastline laid out in front of her. "Oh, Russ, I haven't seen the beach like this for such a long time. It's gorgeous."

"Come on. The view from my front window is just as pretty."

The ice was broken. Whatever had kept him from talking with her on the elevator seemed to disappear. He was back to being his old self. She followed him into a very modern condo done in blue, melon, and greens against a background of cream carpet and walls.

"Gosh, this is so nice."

"You sound surprised. Did you think my daughter and I lived in a dump?"

"Well, no, but this is so well decorated. Did you do it by yourself, or was it like this when you bought it?"

"Yes and no to your two questions. Gayle helped me get started. The house had to be sold in the divorce settlement. I didn't care. I wanted something closer to the hospital. This condo came open, and I've never regretted buying it. I got to know some of the decorators around town, and they made sure I didn't mess up. Decorating and fixing up the place for us became another diversion for me while I watched Libby recuperate."

He pointed to a painting over the couch. "Do you recognize that?"

"That's Horn Island, isn't it?"

"Yep. It's by one of our local artists. Kind of makes you want to go out there again, doesn't it?"

"Oh, yeah."

But Nikki wondered if she'd ever be able to spend a day on his boat again, especially since Libby had become so upset when she saw them kissing. Even thinking about the moment made her face flush.

"I've got to take a quick shower. Could I persuade you to start chopping the vegetables while I'm washing up?"

She turned her back to the sink and leaned against the counter. "Russ, is Libby still upset with us?"

He stuck his hands into his pockets. "I'm not sure that 'upset' is the right way to describe her. I think she's confused. She's her old self most of the time, but then she'll look at me sometimes, and I can see it in her eyes. She doesn't want to share me."

"Have you spoken to her doctor?"

"We've talked about her possessiveness before. He says it'll pass. She's been through so much with the divorce and her surgeries that she's probably emotionally and socially lagging behind some of her classmates. But school's starting soon, and this is the first year she doesn't have a surgery scheduled. We're hoping she'll be so distracted, she won't know I'm in the same house with her."

"Let's hope."

"I have a lot of confidence in Libby. Most little girls couldn't have handled all that she's been through and come out of it with a good attitude. If loving me too much is her only fault, well, then, I think she's done very well."

"I do too." Nikki breathed easier. "Okay, show me your kitchen. I'm dying to start chopping something."

He showed her where everything was and left her alone to work on the vegetables. It felt strange being there. She held the knife still as a wave of apprehension swept over her.

For two years she had avoided anything close to being domestic with anyone.

Being domestic, even washing dishes together, was like changing bed linens. It implied permanence, commitment. That scared her. Could she ever take that step again? She knew that Russ wasn't David, but then, the man David had turned into wasn't the man she had married.

How could she ever be certain again that the things that seemed permanent would stay that way?

But then, she only had to remind herself that her friendship with Russ had never wavered. In all the years she'd known him, he had never changed, only matured.

She pulled the last peel from the onion and cleared the counter before starting to chop. With her mind on Russ, her actions were automatic. Her thoughts floated from her friendship with Russ to his kisses that took away her breath, and from Libby's obvious love of her father to the distrust the girl showed her.

As that thought sent a wave of anxiety through Nikki, Russ returned from the shower. One look at him and her worries vanished.

He stepped up to the counter.

"Hey, you're good," he said as leaned over and eyed her handiwork. "My scampi has never had such beautifully cut onions."

Nikki looked down at the bowl of onions cut into every shape and size, making her remember that her mind had been on other, more important things.

His smile was big when she turned and looked up at him.

"Okay, don't make fun. Variety is good. We couldn't have all these onions cut the same, now, could we?"

He laughed, then reached down and pulled out a heavy skillet. "Doesn't matter how they're cut. It's all the same once I work my magic with this pan."

He asked her to retrieve a few items from his pantry, then pulled out a bar stool. "Now it's my turn. I invited you to dine with me. I want you to sit and talk while I cook."

"But, Russ, I want to help."

"Nope. You're my guest. Please. Let me do this for you."

How could she refuse? She sat and watched him take control of the kitchen.

"You're pretty good at this stuff," she said as he sautéed the onions. "I think you've done this before."

"Yeah, a time or two."

"You cook for lots of women, do you?" She tried to hide a smile.

She watched him frown, then, realizing she was joking, chuckle out loud. "Libby's a little young to call a woman, but she's my best customer."

Then he got serious. "I haven't dated much since the divorce, Nikki. I've taken out a couple of women over the years, but I've never brought one here. Not one of them has met Libby or my family."

That surprised her. "Well, then, I feel special."

He stopped stirring the onions and turned to her. "You are very special."

Leaving her with her mouth hanging open, he turned back to the stove. Unable to hide the mixture of emotions that swept through her, she was glad he had his back to her.

Nothing else personal was said as he whipped up an impressive meal of shrimp scampi, salad, and hot bread. Gayle had come in earlier in the day to put rice into the rice cooker. Russ did the rest.

They ate their meal on the small deck overlooking

the channel. A few boats churned up the water as they made their way back into port, but most of the time the only activity they saw was that of the birds swooping down for an evening meal.

As the sun put on its usual show, they got up from the table and leaned against the railing.

"It's so beautiful," she said.

He turned her to him. Her heart raced as she lifted her face, waiting for the kiss that he hadn't given her earlier. Instead, he brushed the hair away from her forehead and kissed her there. Turning her, he pulled her back close to his body as they watched the final show of the sun.

At first she was confused, wondering why he hadn't kissed her, but as she leaned into his chest, she realized how enjoyable and personal it was to take in the sunset together. She relaxed against him and watched the sun vanish below the horizon.

Afterward she helped Russ clean up the kitchen. They worked well together, she thought. They always had. Even doing mundane chores took on a pleasant feeling. Working side by side, they laughed at each other's corny jokes and talked about life's small hitches. Nothing deep. Nothing world shattering. Simply two people enjoying each other's company.

The evening slipped away before Nikki knew it. With the last of the dishes in the dishwasher and Russ' kitchen sparkling, he took her hand. "Let's go for a walk."

Together they ambled down the beach boardwalk to

a new ice cream parlor. Russ ordered a small banana split.

"Russ, how are we going to eat a banana split? We just had dinner."

"Oh, come on. I've never seen you turn down ice cream. You can't fool me."

She opened her mouth to answer but said nothing. He was right. He knew her too well.

They sat along the seawall, digging into the ice cream with two spoons. After finishing off every last piece of pineapple in the plastic bowl, they removed their shoes and walked to the water's edge.

The moon's glow sparkled on the waves as Russ held her hand. The quiet beauty of the evening settled around her. She thought that it would be another perfect moment for a kiss, but as she looked up at Russ, she realized she didn't need a kiss. Just being with him thrilled her.

They walked and talked. Every once in a while he'd pick up a shell in the sand and throw it out over the water. He was a perfect gentleman, making her feel like the woman she'd forgotten she was.

"I've enjoyed this, Russ. Thank you for a wonderful evening," she said as he walked her to her car. "I hate for the night to end."

"Me too." He opened the car door for her.

After tossing her purse onto the seat, she turned to him. Before she could say any more, he placed his hands on both her shoulders, pulled her to him, and kissed her lips. Not hard, not in a passionate embrace, but soft and gentle.

Her knees weakened when he pulled away just far enough for her to see his face.

"I had a wonderful time too, Nikki. Can we do this again?"

She only nodded. Her head still spun from the kiss. As she got behind the wheel, he leaned down with his arms crossed on the window.

"Call me when you get home. I'll feel better knowing you got there safely." Then he grinned. "I'm not used to sending *all* my women off in their own cars."

She was still grinning as she pulled away.

Chapter Twelve

Nikki slipped her cell phone into her purse. Russ had asked her to pick up Libby and Hammerhead from Gayle's and then to meet him at the boat after work. Several days had gone by since their dinner together. Nikki looked forward to seeing him again but had her reservations.

His request sounded simple enough, but knowing how Libby resented her, she hoped the girl would get into her car.

"Maybe it's best I didn't have children. I probably wouldn't know how to raise one." But as soon as the words escaped her lips, she knew that wasn't true.

She loved children. Longed for a daughter of her own. Dreamed of giving a husband a son to be proud of.

"Phooey, Nikki. You sure know how to make yourself miserable," she muttered.

She snatched up her purse and headed to work, looking forward to being with Russ and his daughter later in the day. She could only hope Libby would come around.

The day flew by, and by 5:15 Nikki pulled up in front of Gayle's house. Everything looked peaceful, but as soon as she stepped out of the car, she heard Libby calling Hammerhead's name. Gayle's voice, then both of her boys' voices, followed.

Nikki saw the little group coming down the sidewalk. Gayle held Libby's hand. The two boys marched behind them.

The strained look on Gayle's face told Nikki that something wasn't right.

"Thank goodness, you're here," Gayle said as Nikki stepped out of the car. "It's my turn in the car pool to take about five boys to gym class, and Libby's in a state. We can't find Hammerhead."

Nikki knelt down by Libby.

Libby swiped her hand across her eyes. "Hammerhead ran away. He couldn't go with Daddy today, so we kept him. But he ran away. Even he doesn't like me."

Nikki looked up at Gayle, who shrugged, then stooped down next to Libby. "That's not true," Gayle said. "Hammerhead loves you. We all do."

"Of course he does. I've seen how excited he gets

when he sees you," Nikki chimed in. "He doesn't wag that tail for just anyone."

Libby's bottom lip quivered. "Yeah, he wags his tail. And sometimes he licks me all over."

"See? That shows how much he loves you." Nikki turned to Gayle. "When did you notice he was gone?"

"He was in the yard all day like he always is when he's here, but when it was time to get the boys ready, maybe thirty minutes ago, I realized he wasn't here. Looks like he dug under the back fence."

"Oh, my. Where've you looked?"

"Only on this block. Do you think you could take Libby around the next block to look for him? I'll drop the boys off at class, then come back to help. I won't be long."

"By all means. We'll try our best to find him." Nikki looked down at Libby. "He probably saw a friend he wanted to play with."

"Really?"

Libby's tear-filled eyes crashed right into Nikki's heart. She cleared her throat before answering. "Sounds like that might be the case. Come on. Let's go look for him."

She reached for Libby's hand, but the little girl crossed her arms in front of herself. Nikki pushed away the usual wave of hurt when Libby refused to respond to her.

"You take the boys, Gayle. Libby and I will do our best to find him. I'll call you if we have any luck."

Gayle drove off with the boys, leaving Nikki alone

with Libby. "Come on, let's walk this way first. Then, if we don't find him, we'll come back and take the car."

Libby nodded and started walking, calling Hammerhead's name. Nikki tried whistling, calling, and saying a few silent prayers.

She knew this wasn't her fault, but she had a feeling that if Hammerhead wasn't located, Russ' daughter would somehow blame her for it.

How she wanted to take the child into her arms and comfort her. Libby's brown eyes still showed signs of tears, and an occasional sniffle drifted up to Nikki, but she knew better than to force herself on the girl. She simply prayed they'd find Hammerhead.

The two of them walked around the neighborhood, first one street and then another. With each step Nikki felt more and more discouraged. Gayle lived only one block away from the busy beach highway. She wouldn't let herself think about what could've happened if the dog had run out into the traffic.

Finally they rounded another corner. "Libby, I think we need to go back to the house. Hammerhead might be there. Sometimes dogs just like to wander around, but they come home when they get hungry."

Libby sniffled. "Okay."

Nikki caught the trembling of the girl's bottom lip and couldn't control herself. She knelt down and pulled the little girl into her arms.

Libby didn't pull away. In fact, she snuggled into Nikki's arms and held on tightly.

"I love Hammerhead. I don't want him to go away."

"I know you do, and he loves you too. I've seen the way he follows you around. He'll be okay. Come on, let's keep calling."

She squeezed Libby a little closer to her before letting her go.

"Hammerhead, where are you?" Libby called as she walked next to Nikki.

Nikki took a chance and reached for her hand.

Libby took it.

Nikki wanted to shout for joy. Instead, she called Hammerhead's name and then put two fingers to her lips and whistled as loudly as she could.

Libby looked up and giggled. "That's as loud as some of the boys at school whistle."

"Yep. I learned that from my dad. My mother thought it wasn't very ladylike, but Dad was real proud of me."

Libby seemed to like that. She put her fingers to her lips and tried. Nikki showed her how to hold her fingers, then let her practice before starting their hunt once again.

Knowing they were getting close to Gayle's block, Nikki yelled Hammerhead's name one last time, then whistled.

She stopped. "Was that a bark?"

Libby had heard it too. "Hammerhead? Where are you?"

Again and again they called out his name until the bark was clearly close to them.

Finally Nikki saw him. Sitting behind a tall chain-link fence, Hammerhead watched them walk toward him. With tail wagging and tongue hanging out, he looked happy to see them.

Libby tugged at Nikki's hand, trying to run. "Hammerhead, what are you doing in that yard?"

But then the answer became clear. From around the corner of the house pranced a medium-sized dog with a coat of long white fur. Nikki couldn't tell for sure, but she had a feeling this dog was female.

"Look, Miss Nikki. Hammerhead has a friend!"

"He sure does."

She opened the gate. Hammerhead jumped up on her, let her rub his head, then immediately turned his attention to Libby. The girl laughed out loud as his big tongue licked her hands.

"Hammerhead, you're a bad dog. We were scared you'd run away."

"But he's okay."

Nikki walked up to the front door and knocked. An older woman opened the door. After a pleasant greeting, she looked at Libby and the dog.

"Is that big dog yours?" she asked the girl.

"Yes," Nikki answered. "I'm afraid he escaped from her aunt's yard."

"I saw where he dug under the fence in the back, but he looked so ferocious that I was scared to make him leave. Anyway, my Princess seemed to like him, so I guess he didn't do any harm."

"I hope not. Here." Nikki gave the lady her phone number. "If you need someone to fix the fence or anything else he might have harmed, please call me, and I'll see that it's done. He's not my dog, but his owner is very responsible."

"Thank you, but I already called my son. He said he'd be by to see if I need anything. I'm sure everything will be okay."

"Come on, Hammerhead. You've given us a big scare."

The walk home seemed much shorter and a lot more pleasant than the last thirty minutes had. With Hammerhead and Libby running and bouncing in front of her, Nikki followed with a smile on her face.

After calling Gayle with the good news and herding Hammerhead into the backseat of her car, Nikki turned to Libby. "Let's take him home. Your dad will be thrilled to see both of you."

Libby put her face against a back window. Hammerhead licked it from the inside. Nikki didn't care that she'd just paid to have the car detailed. Hammerhead was going home with Libby. Nothing could ruin her day.

She touched Libby's shoulder. "Come on. We might get to the harbor in time to see your dad come down the channel."

Libby turned around, stood still a minute, then threw her arms around Nikki's legs. "Thank you, Miss Nikki. You helped me find our dog."

Shock and joy raced through Nikki's veins. She

reached down and stroked Libby' s hair, pulled up in a ponytail.

"I'm so glad we did. I think he heard you call him. He recognized your voice. That's what I think."

"Really?"

"Oh, most definitely. Dogs know who loves them."

With a last quick squeeze to Nikki's legs, Libby spun around and climbed into the front seat.

Nikki had to take a moment to breathe before going around to her side of the car. Then she skipped around the rear of the car, stopping only to look into the window at the huge mound of fur that sat with his back haunches on the seat, his front paws hanging over the front, and saliva drooling down from his mouth.

She'd never seen anything so beautiful.

Chapter Thirteen

School started early in south Mississippi. By late of August Libby had settled into a routine, and, according to Russ's phone calls, she seemed to love her new teacher and was adjusting well.

Phone calls had been the extent of their contact since the incident with Hammerhead. With the fall fishing season beginning, the charter business escalated and kept Russ on the water and Nikki behind her desk. So, that day when he called and asked if she could get away for a couple of hours, Nikki wasn't about to refuse.

She managed to complete her work early and waited not so patiently for him to pick her up at the office. His early-morning call had kept her wondering what he had planned for the afternoon. Except to tell her to dress for the boat, he'd cut the conversation short.

Dressing wasn't a problem. Most of what she wore to work would be appropriate for a boat as well.

At about three o'clock the door flew open, and Russ stepped in, wearing a grin that was as bright as his yellow boat shirt.

"Ready?"

"I'm ready," she answered, "but I'm not sure for what."

She waited a moment, thinking Russ would shed some light on his plans. Instead, he simply held open the door.

"Well, if you're ready, let's go."

Her mouth opened to protest his secretive approach to their afternoon, but she grabbed her purse and followed him out the door instead. This wasn't David not wanting to share his thoughts. This was Russ, who had planned something special for her. What could it be? The grin that had greeted her still spread across his face as he drove down the beach highway.

Within minutes they were at the harbor. Hammerhead must have heard the truck, because she spotted his big black body heading for the bow of the boat as soon as they pulled up.

"I think he's been waiting for us, and he probably knows more than I do about what we're doing here in the middle of the week."

Russ chuckled as he opened the door. "Dogs are smart that way."

Nikki followed him onto the boat. "Hi, Hammerhead. You haven't run off anymore, have you?" Hammerhead rubbed against her leg, waiting for his expected petting. Nikki reached down and rubbed his head, then helped Russ with the lines. Without another word about where they were going, she made herself comfortable on the bridge alongside Russ.

Chitchat was easy. It always was with Russ. She asked about Libby's school and about Mrs. Preston and about the boys. At times Russ was talkative, but then, as the boat headed south from the eastern channel, he seemed pensive.

"Looks like we're heading for Horn Island."

"You're right. I thought you'd like to visit the island after you spotted it on our fishing trip."

"So that's my surprise destination?"

"Yeah. Disappointed?"

"Of course not. I'm thrilled. How could I be disappointed when a very handsome man has planned to take me to the most gorgeous spot on the coast?"

He answered her with another smile and pushed the throttle forward. *The Half-Moon* flew across the water, leaving a trail as straight as a pin behind them. The afternoon was what Nikki called a chamber-of-commerce day, the kind of day you prayed to have when special visitors were coming to town: bright sunshine, a light breeze, and water that reflected the deep azure sky.

Sitting on the bridge with Russ, Nikki took in her surroundings and once again knew she'd made the right decision to come home. What more could she possibly want?

Within minutes she could see the tree line along the eastern shore of the island; then, as if a painter had passed his brush along the southern horizon, the white sand beach appeared.

"There it is!" She placed a hand on Russ' knee. "Thank you for asking me."

Russ looked down at her hand before answering. "My pleasure. I'm glad you came. I took a chance asking you in the middle of the week, but I knew today was too perfect to waste in an office."

Russ chose a spot along the northern shore where the water was deep enough for him to pull the boat up against the beach. Hammerhead wasted no time in jumping off the boat. Soon they followed him down the beach, walking hand in hand along the water's edge. With the waves lapping gently against her feet and the afternoon sun warming her shoulders, Nikki felt young and free.

She stooped to pick up a shell. "Look, Russ. Look how perfect it is. Not even a chip. It's beautiful."

As she held it up for him to see, he touched it, then put his hands on her shoulders. "But not as beautiful as you."

She wanted to make a joke about his compliment, but when she looked up into his eyes, she was shocked to see how serious he was.

He placed a finger over her lips. "Don't tell me that I'm crazy for telling you how beautiful you are. When I look at you, I see someone with a beauty that reaches way beyond the surface."

"You're being much too kind, Russ. You really are."

"Am I? I don't think so." He nodded toward a log half covered in the sand. "Come over here. Let's sit. I want to talk."

Pushing away the sand on the top of the log, she made them a clean place to sit, but when she sat, she was alone. Russ remained standing.

She watched him reach into his shorts' pocket and pull out a small box. "This is for you—if you'll take it."

The gold box with black embossed lettering came from a local jeweler. "You bought me a gift? What's the occasion?"

"There isn't an occasion—not yet. Open it, Nikki."

She took the box, ran her fingers along the lettering, and savored their rich feel. "I love gifts, but I'm at a loss about why . . ." Her words trailed off as she opened the lid to reveal a diamond ring tucked within black velvet.

Her mouth dropped open, but no words came. She pulled her gaze away from the ring to look at Russ. "Is this what I think it is?"

"I hope so." Russ knelt in front of her and took her hand. "Nikki, I didn't think I would ever marry again. I couldn't imagine ever wanting to share Libby's and my life with anyone. But then you walked back into my world, and now I can't think of anything else."

Nikki looked down at the ring again. Her breath hitched. "I—I don't know what to say. I had no idea."

"I know. This hasn't been the most romantic courtship,

but I've felt pulled in a million directions. You have to believe me, though, when I say you've never left my mind." He put his hand over his heart. "Or my heart. You've been right here the entire time."

He cleared his throat. "I didn't think I could ever love again, but I do. I love you. You've turned my life around. I haven't been unhappy for the last couple of years—Libby and I have a good life—but I've been missing something, and you've given that something back to me. I want to do the same for you. Say you'll marry me."

"This is so fast."

"No, it isn't. We've known each other for years."

"You know what I mean. I've been working so hard not to ruin our friendship that I wouldn't allow myself to look beyond that. I was scared to think it possible that you felt the same way. Scared you saw me only as a friend."

"Then you do love me."

Nikki's heart pounded. "I do. I love you."

"Then say you'll marry me."

"I want to, Russ, but what about Libby? I could never marry you unless there was hope that she could come to love me too."

Russ pulled her into a tight embrace. "Believe me, she already loves you."

"She knows about what you're doing?"

"She knows."

"Then, what can I say? Yes. Yes, I'll marry you."

His kiss left no room for doubt. She had come home in more ways than one.

Russ kept the boat on a slow, steady run all the way home. "I don't want this afternoon to end. I'm scared if I get you home too fast, this will all have been a dream."

Nikki reached over and placed a hand over his on the steering wheel. "It's not a dream. At least I hope it's not. You can let *The Half-Moon* go as fast as she can."

With that, he opened the throttle, and the boat flew across the water. "Glad you suggested that. We still have one more thing to do."

"I guess I can't ask what that might be."

"You can ask . . ."

She finished it for him. "But you won't answer. I get it. Well, if I can't ask about that, may I ask you something else?"

"Sure."

"From the first day that I saw your boat's name on my list, I wondered why it was named after a half-moon. Why didn't you call her *The Full Moon* or something like that?"

He rested his hand on the wheel as if remembering the joy that his boat had brought him. "It wasn't a big decision, naming her. A full moon is the ultimate, the limit. There's nothing to look forward to except the waning. With a half-moon, you know that bigger and better things are in store. I had to be hopeful. My boat and my daughter gave me that hope."

Nikki thought about his words. *Half-moon.* A better future. Something to look forward to. She smiled and leaned into his arms, savoring the feeling of love. "I really like that. You named her just right."

As they neared the mainland, Russ called Gayle on his cell phone. "We'll be at the harbor in about ten minutes."

When he hung up, Nikki shook her head. "Yes, I know—don't ask."

This time he laughed.

Gayle's minivan, filled with several extra little boys, was parked in the harbor. Gayle helped Libby out and escorted her to the pier, where Russ met them. Gayle left after Russ took Libby's hand.

Russ jumped back onto the deck of the boat, then reached out and helped Libby board. A small cloth bag with a string was tied around her wrist.

Nikki wanted to reach out and hug her, but as soon as Libby's feet touched the deck, the little girl backed up against the railing and looked down at her shoes. Nikki's heart sank. She looked at Russ for reassurance, but before he answered, Hammerhead rubbed up against Libby's legs.

"Hey, boy. Did you go to the island?" the girl asked.

Nikki spoke up. "He did, and he had a good time. I wish you could've been with us."

Libby looked up at Russ.

"We all had a good time. The next time we want you to go with us—as a family."

Libby shrugged and petted Hammerhead. "That would be fun."

For an awkward moment all three of them stood silently.

Russ finally spoke up. "Don't you want to tell Miss Nikki something?"

Libby nodded but didn't say anything. She shuffled onto one foot and then the other. "Yes, sir."

Libby looked up at Nikki. "Daddy told me that he wanted you to be my mama."

Nikki knelt down in front of her. "He did, and with all my heart I want you to be my little girl."

She pulled Libby to her chest and held her tightly. "Libby, I've never had a little girl. I've never had any children, but I think I could learn to be your mother." She held her at arm's length. "I would try really hard if you'll give me a chance. I love your daddy, and I want us to be a family."

Libby looked up at Russ once more.

Russ nodded.

Libby stepped back and fumbled with the string around her wrist.

Russ stooped down and helped to loosen the string. Libby reached into the bag and pulled out a small ring box and pushed it in Nikki's direction. "It's another ring. I want you to wear it if you're going to be my mama."

The significance of wearing the child's ring swelled Nikki's heart.

"If you'll let me be part of your family, I'd love to wear your ring. It would be very special to me.

"I want you to wear this like you're wearing Daddy's."

Nikki took the box. When she opened it, instead of the toy ring that she anticipated, she recognized the ring that MaryAnn had worn for years, an heirloom from the Preston family. Its large ruby surrounded by diamonds still glimmered as brightly as the day that MaryAnn had proudly shown it to Nikki years ago.

"Mama gave me this ring when she left. She told me it was mine now, but she said it was Daddy's mama's before that and *her* mama's before that. So now it's mine, and if it's mine, I told Daddy that I could do anything with it, and I wanted you to have it." She caught her breath before finishing. "That way, if you wear it, you might stay with me and Daddy forever."

Nikki couldn't find words.

Russ stooped down beside them. "Nikki, this was Libby's idea. I couldn't tell her no. Do you mind—you know—with the history of this ring and all?"

Nikki understood perfectly what he was saying, since his former wife had worn it.

"Do I mind?" Nikki took the ring out of the box and slipped it onto her right hand. "I have the two most beautiful rings in the world from two of the most beautiful people in the world." She pulled Libby into her arms. "Sweetheart, you and your daddy have made me feel like the luckiest person ever. I love your daddy, and

I want to be his wife, and I want to be your mother—forever. I love you."

Russ put his arms around the two of them. Nothing had ever felt more right to Nikki.

By the time they climbed off the boat, the sun had set, and the sky was dark. Russ held his daughter in one arm and held Nikki's hand with the other. At the end of the pier he stopped and nodded toward the eastern sky.

"The moon's coming up. If I'm not mistaken, it won't be a very big one tonight. I think it's only a half-moon." He looked at Nikki and winked.

Libby looked up. "Look, Miss Nikki. The moon is like the fish I threw back. It's not big enough yet. It's got to grow."

"Yes, and it will." Nikki looked at Russ. "Just like our love."

Then both of them laughed as Libby threw a kiss to the sky and shouted, "Go grow, moon!"